KU-304-154

12/22

£1.50

The Outside Child

The Outside Child

NINA BAWDEN

LONDON
VICTOR GOLLANCZ LTD
1989

For Pat, with love

First published in Great Britain 1989
by Victor Gollancz Ltd,
14 Henrietta Street, London WC2E 8QJ

Copyright © Nina Bawden 1989

British Library Cataloguing in Publication Data
Bawden, Nina
    The outside child.
    I. Title
    823'.914 [J]

ISBN 0-575-04601-5

Photoset in Great Britain by
Rowland Phototypesetting Ltd, Bury St Edmunds, Suffolk
and printed by St Edmundsbury Press Ltd
Bury St Edmunds, Suffolk

Chapter One

I am an outside child. That is what Plato Jones calls me.

Plato is my best friend in the world, even though I am a bit ashamed to be seen with him sometimes. He is a year younger than I am, only twelve, and small and thin for his age. He wears braces on his teeth that make him spit when he talks, and huge, goggly glasses, and he can't run or play games because of his asthma. He says, "Only another outside child would put up with me." He says we are both like the Bisto Kids—raggedy kids in an old advertisement, standing out in the cold and peering in through a window at a warm kitchen where someone's mother is cooking.

My mother is dead. She died just after I was born, and because my father is a marine engineer, away at sea most of the time, Aunt Sophie and Aunt Bill (whose name is Wilhemina) looked after me. They are my father's second cousins and their mothers were twin sisters who died on the same day. In our family, the mothers die early.

This sounds as if it could be a sad story. But I am not a sad person, though sometimes people think that I ought to be. Like the smiling lady who came from the court when I was adopted. She asked lots of questions and she smiled as she asked them and smiled as I answered. She was trying to find out if I really wanted to be adopted by Aunt Bill and Aunt Sophie.

She said, "Wouldn't you like to live in a proper family, Jane? A family with a Mummy and Daddy?"

I was seven years old. I thought it was silly for her to say

Mummy and *Daddy* as if I were still a baby. I said, "I can't, can I? My mother is dead and my father is busy."

"I know that, Jane dear," she said. She had stopped smiling and was looking so serious that I wanted to giggle.

I knew that I mustn't. I stared at her, making my eyes go out of focus so that her face became blurry. I said, "I'm quite happy as I am, thank you."

"Child's not a fool," Aunt Bill said, and laughed the loud, barking laugh that meant she was nervous. She has a round, flat face like a dinner plate and it was suddenly shiny and damp as if it had been dipped into water. She had changed out of her jeans and her old fisherman's smock for this visit, and put on a pretty skirt with purple flowers on it, and a clean, cotton shirt, but she still looked wild as a gipsy, with her thick, curly hair standing up stiff as the garden broom and her bare, knobbly feet a bit dirty.

I saw the adoption lady glance at them—a quick look, not long enough to be rude, but long enough to make me wish Aunt Bill had put a pair of shoes on. Then she said, "Well, you do seem to know your own mind Miss Jane Tucker!"

And although she had started smiling again, I knew she was sorry for me because I wanted to stay with these two funny old ladies.

I only say *funny* and *old* because I could see that was what she thought about them.

Aunt Bill is an artist. She paints bright, splashy pictures of fruit and flowers—of all the things, even the weeds, that grow in our garden. Aunt Sophie teaches the piano, and plays the drums in a band. She is very little, shorter than me by the time I was ten: Aunt Bill says she must be the world's smallest drummer. But she is very fierce and quick; when she is rushing around cooking or cleaning Aunt Bill takes care to keep out of her way. Aunt Sophie won't let Aunt Bill do a thing in the house because she is so clumsy and slow, and Aunt Bill won't let Aunt Sophie touch a single growing thing in the garden. "Too impatient," she says. "If a plant isn't doing well, Sophie will grub it up to see why. She'd never think of encouraging it to do better, the way she would a young human creature, a child at the piano."

Aunt Bill encourages her plants. "There, little darling," she says as she pricks out a seedling. "Push out your roots and make yourself comfy."

If Aunt Sophie hears her, she purses her mouth and rolls her eyes up to Heaven. But she doesn't often hear what other people say unless she is actually having a conversation with them: most of the time she is too busy listening to the music playing inside her head. Like someone with an invisible Walkman.

Writing this down makes them both seem pretty weird. But I've always lived with them, and they seem normal to me. And lots of people are adopted. There's nothing odd about that. Nothing to put you *outside*. Or not on its own, Plato says.

Just after my thirteenth birthday, Aunt Sophie took me to the docks to meet my father's ship. He is Chief Engineer on a big passenger liner that once went on real voyages to Australia and back again, but since everyone flies nowadays because it is quicker and cheaper, the ship takes people on holiday cruises instead. "A bit of a come-down," Aunt Bill calls it. "It's no way to treat a great ship, to turn it into a floating fun palace. Undignified. Rather as if you took a proud and stately old woman and made her caper about in a short frilly dress and a silly hat."

I know ships are alive to Aunt Bill, just like plants; all the same, I think she is sometimes a bit over-fanciful. It seemed to me, standing on the dock with Aunt Sophie, that my father's ship was still fine and beautiful as it came slowly in, and the passengers, hanging over the side and waving to their families and friends who had come to meet them, looked healthy and happy. I said to Aunt Sophie, "I don't think the ship looks like an old woman, do you?"

"No more than this old woman looks like a ship." Aunt Sophie tapped her skinny chest with her knuckles. "Turn Bill's nonsense around and you'll see it for what it is." She sniffed. "Arty farty sentimentality. Don't you let yourself be taken in by it, Jane. Things are just *things*. Nothing like *people*."

I said, "My father says ships are like women. They like their own way. He calls his ship *she*."

I was teasing her. Aunt Sophie thinks my father is wonderful. She blushed; her forehead and cheeks and little owlish hooked nose, all went the same sunset pink. She said, "That's quite different. Your father's a sailor."

I suppose I think my father is wonderful, too, though I try to hide it. And perhaps now I am older I don't think he is quite as wonderful as I thought he was that Saturday morning, standing on the dockside with Aunt Sophie and looking for him on the deck.

I couldn't see him at first and I began to feel dreadfully shaky; my heart banging about and my knees going rubbery. Aunt Sophie took my hand and squeezed it a couple of times without saying anything and that helped a bit. But when I did see him I was too shy to wave. I screwed up my eyes and pretended I couldn't see very clearly. Aunt Sophie jabbed my ribs with her sharp elbow, "If you're going blind we'd better go straight to the hospital."

"I had something in my eye," I said. "I can feel it's gone now."

I felt everyone watching me as I went up the gangway. Aunt Sophie was in front of me and a sliver of petticoat was drooping under her skirt. I worried about that, about whether I should tell her or if it would be more comfortable for her not to know. Then she was at the top, and calling out, "Edward, how *nice*," and I heard him laugh as he swung her up, and set her down on the deck. He was still laughing as he turned to me, but I didn't want the tail-end of a laugh meant for someone else, so I didn't smile.

He said, "Why, it's my favourite daughter!" raising his eyebrows and pretending to be astonished to see me, and I couldn't help smiling then. He hugged me and kissed me, a bit of a bristly kiss, and held me away, and looked at me carefully; and I looked back at him. He was very brown except for the white lines around his blue eyes where he crinkled them against the sun, and he looked very smart in his gold-braided uniform. I said, "I believe you've grown," which was a joke we had between us from when I was small and thought this was the polite thing to say when you met someone you hadn't seen for a while, because it was what grown-ups always seemed to be saying to me. He gave me another hug and said that I hadn't exactly shrunk, but that the only way he was likely to grow at his age, was sideways.

We went to his cabin. The ship had been cruising down the African coast and he had brought us African presents: necklaces and belts and little dolls made of beads; a big blue and white cloth to use as a bedspread or to hang on a wall, and a small African drum made of animal skin. Because he had just missed my birthday he had brought me an especially beautiful present: a pair of delicate storks, each carved out of an antelope horn.

He poured drinks for us—a pink gin for himself, sherry for Aunt Sophie, and a Coke for me. I had never been allowed Coke at home because of my teeth, and I had grown out of liking or wanting it, but he didn't know that, and I didn't tell him.

He and Aunt Sophie started to talk about African music. Aunt Bill says I developed an allergy to music when I was a baby and Aunt Sophie used to take me to gigs with her and keep me beside her in my carry-cot while she thumped away at the drums and percussion. Whatever the cause, African music is not a subject of great interest to me, and so I

9

went on a tour of inspection around the cabin to see if there was anything new since I had last been there.

There is not much room for change in a cabin because most of the furniture is fixed to the floor so it won't roll about in a storm. This makes for tidiness, too, and my father's cabin was always very neat—the dark wood and all the brass fittings polished and gleaming. The bunk bed was made up with clean sheets and a thick, scarlet blanket, the table had a ledge all around it to stop things sliding off, and there were brass clips fixed to the walls to hold the doors still when they were open. My father's desk was covered with leather that had a wavy band of gold round the edge.

I liked to close my eyes and run my finger along it to feel the shape of the pattern. There were inkwells with brass tops and a brass tray for his pens, and photographs in silver frames. Apart from Aunt Bill and Aunt Sophie—Aunt Sophie at her piano, and Aunt Bill on her knees by a flower bed, and squinting up into the camera and laughing—I didn't know the people in these pictures because most of my father's family had emigrated years ago, to America, and Australia. But I knew them from their photographs. There were my father's parents: his mother very pretty and young, with dark hair pulled back, sitting down and holding a fat baby, who was my father; her husband, a tall man with a black moustache, standing beside her and looking down at them both. There was my father's Uncle Willy, who had been killed in the last war and whose picture had been taken in his army uniform, and his Aunt Alba, Uncle Willy's sister, who had married an American soldier and gone to live in South Carolina and who had two sons and three daughters. I liked Aunt Alba best of them all. She was plump and jolly-looking and she seemed to be smiling straight at me.

I always said hallo to all these people when I came to see my father—not aloud, just silently, in my head—and although it sounds stupid, I imagined they knew I was there and that I was one of their family.

Today, there was a new picture. It was of a girl and a smaller boy, both of them younger than I was. Their picture had not been there before—I was sure of that—and yet, somehow, I felt that I knew them. The girl had long, curly hair, and her eyes were screwed up as if she were nervous of having her photograph taken. The boy was laughing straight at the camera, very bold and sweet. One of his front teeth was missing.

I picked up the picture and said, "Who are they?"

My father and Aunt Sophie turned in the same moment. And they both seemed to freeze—as if I had held a frame in a video.

Then my father made a funny sound, half a sneeze, half a cough.

Aunt Sophie said, "Oh, Edward, how careless!"

He looked very bright-eyed; a bit sly and embarrassed. He said, "Sorry . . ."

Aunt Sophie said, "You'd better explain to her, Edward."

She looked at him, waiting. But he didn't speak, only sighed. She said, "Oh, all right!" She turned to me and said in a funny, flat voice, "Their names are Annabel and George. Annabel is your father's other daughter and George is his son. So they are your half brother and sister."

It was the most exciting thing that had ever happened to me. One minute I was an only child, the next I was a big sister. Of course, *that* was why I had felt that I knew them! Since we were relations we must look a bit alike! Even though my hair wasn't curly like Annabel's I knew that I screwed my eyes up sometimes, just as she had done for this picture. And the way George was laughing, his mouth stretched so wide that it pushed up little fat pads on his cheekbones, reminded me of my father.

Perhaps it is strange that I didn't ask why I hadn't been told about them before. But I didn't even wonder about it—or not at that moment. All I wanted just then was to find out all about them; how old they were, and what sort of people, and what they liked doing. My father was slow to answer. He seemed nervous, almost shy of me, suddenly. But after a little he went to his desk and took a photograph album out of a drawer.

Annabel was ten years old, and George was seven. "A young rapscallion," my father said. "If there's hot water anywhere, he'll be the first in it. Leap first and look second, that's George! Annabel's more the cautious type. Dreamier. She reads a lot, well ahead of her age in that department her teacher says, but her chief talent is music. She's doing remarkably well with the French horn."

He sounded proud, Aunt Sophie looked interested, and I was jealous. Then I remembered that my father had called me his 'favourite' daughter. As I had thought that I was the only one, it had just seemed one of his jokes. Now I thought perhaps he had meant it! But I wasn't sure that I wanted him to like me better than Annabel. I loved her more and more as I looked at her photographs and she looked back at me with her funny, worried smile that she had had ever since she was a round, dimply baby.

I loved George, too. No one could help it. He looked so cheeky and always as if he were just about to do something naughty. *Catch me if you can*, was what he seemed to be saying in most of his pictures.

I was full of love for them both. I said, "If you tell me when their birthdays are, I can send them presents."

My father said nothing. Aunt Sophie had a gathered-up look on her face, as if she were pursing her feelings up tight.

I knew I had said something wrong, though I didn't know what it was. I turned the next page of the album. There was a picture of George as a fat toddler, running and looking back over his shoulder and laughing at a lady who was running after him. She was wearing a billowy skirt and her long hair was tied in a pony-tail. She was the only grown-up in the album and I supposed that she must be George's mother.

I hadn't thought about the mother before. And as soon as I did think about her, I thought about something else. And it made me feel very odd. I said, "Is that your wife, Dad?" I hoped that my voice sounded ordinary.

He seemed to take a hundred years to answer. When he did, his voice sounded carefully casual, rather as I hoped mine had done. "Yes, it is. I took that particular picture. Amy took all the others. At different times, of course. Then made a book of them for me."

My ears sang. I said—I knew before I spoke that it was stupid, but I still had to say it—"I didn't know you were married."

Aunt Sophie said softly, "Oh, Jane!"

And my father laughed abruptly. His tanned cheeks had flushed darker. "But of course you knew, silly girl!"

Aunt Sophie said, "It was a long time ago, Edward. She was very small. It's not something we've talked about since."

"No," my father said. "No, I suppose not."

None of this made any sense to me. I was ashamed to say that I didn't understand. I said, "I expect you did tell me and I forgot." This sounded dreadful. How could you forget that your father was married? I hit myself on the forehead and said in a loud, cheerful voice, "I've got a memory like a sieve sometimes."

Neither of them smiled as I had intended. They were both looking guilty and sorrowful, which was idiotic, I thought. After all, it wasn't as if I had discovered some terrible secret like my father being a drug smuggler or something! I said, "I'm *glad* I've got a brother and sister. When can I see them?"

Aunt Sophie sighed. My father said, "Well, we'll have to

think about that! Not just now, though. Lunch is the next item on the agenda." He got up, suddenly very brisk and hearty, and looked at Aunt Sophie. He said, "You'll sort it out, won't you?"

And Aunt Sophie sighed again.

"It's all very difficult for your father," Aunt Sophie shouted.

She had to shout because we were driving home in Rattlebones. Rattlebones is our car, and the name tells you all that you need to know about it except that even with dozens of cushions Aunt Sophie is still too small to look over the steering wheel and has to look through it. This means she is too small to be seen from the outside as well, and Rattlebones, wheezing and banging along with no one apparently driving, is an awesome sight.

I saw at least six people look at us with horror as we lurched down the High Street.

I said—I could say it now—"I don't see why no one told me."

"I expect we thought you'd be upset," Aunt Sophie said.

"I don't see why. I'm not upset now!"

Aunt Sophie sighed. She was in one of her sighing moods.

I thought I knew what was bothering her. I said, kindly, "It's all right. I don't want to leave home and go to live with them. I'm your girl, and Aunt Bill's. But I could go and see them sometimes. I could play with them and teach them things."

"It isn't so simple," Aunt Sophie said. We were through the shopping street now. She turned into a side road by the edge of the school playing fields and stopped Rattlebones with a jerk and a squeal as she put on the handbrake. The silence was lovely.

Aunt Sophie sat still for a minute. She was still hanging on to the steering wheel—so tight that her knuckles showed white. She said, "Their mother doesn't want them to see you. And she doesn't want you to see them. They don't know about you and she wants to keep it that way. She knows your father loves you just as much as he loves Annabel and George, but she likes to think they are his only children. As I said, it's hard on your father. But he thought, we all thought, that since that was how Amy felt, it was best you didn't know anything either. At least, not until you were older." She took a hand off the steering wheel and let it rest on my knee.

I said, "But their photograph was there, on his desk. He knows I always go and look at the photographs." I remembered something. "You said he was careless."

Another little puffing sigh. "I suppose he usually tucks it away in a drawer when you're coming."

"And what about my photograph? Does he put that away when *they* come?"

"Probably. Turn and turnabout." She took off her driving glasses and rubbed at the red mark they had left on her nose. "What a silly game!"

I felt very strange. Annabel and George didn't know about me, and unless my father—*our* father, that is!—was "careless" again, they might never know. Nothing had changed for them. But everything had changed for me. The world had grown bigger. It was as if I had found another room in the house that I lived in, a secret locked room, and was looking through a window at the children who played there. Only I couldn't play with them. I couldn't even talk to them. They couldn't hear me. They couldn't see my face at the window.

It was as if I had suddenly become an invisible person.

Chapter Two

I rang Plato. "Swen," I said. "Sti tnatropmi. Teem em? Yako?"

"Gnah tuoba," he said.

There was a clatter as he dropped the telephone receiver and a crash as he knocked over something. Then the thud of his feet up the passage and the soapy music as he opened the sitting room door—either the beginning or the end of one of the television serials his mother was hooked on. I hoped it was the beginning and it must have been, because I didn't have to hang about long. He was back. "Yako. Si ti dab swen?"

"On. Ton dab swen, tub tnatropmi." I wanted to say 'exciting', or 'fascinating', but both those words are impossible to pronounce backwards in a hurry. Or, rather, I couldn't be bothered. We had to play this childish back-speak game because of Plato's mother, who had nothing better to do than eavesdrop on other people. We used a substitution code when we wrote to each other, which is more interesting, but difficult for conversation. "Lausu ecalp," I said. "Yako?"

"Yako, Enaj."

I must tell you how I met Plato. He goes to my school. He is in the year below mine which is embarrassing, sometimes, because most girls have boy friends who are older than they are. Not that Plato is my boy friend. He is a friend who happens to be a boy.

I got to know him when I had trouble with a girl called Maureen. She lives next door and she is the same age as me, so at one time her mother was always dumping her over the fence into our garden. Nice for Jane to have a little friend, was what she said, meaning that it was convenient for her. I hated Maureen from the beginning. She hid my toys to tease me, and stole my best felt tip pens, and pulled my hair when no one was looking. The worst thing of all was when she found my private notebook and read out my poems in a loud, sniggery voice. I could have killed her for that. I punched her in the face and she fell over backwards and screamed until Aunt Bill came running.

And, naturally, Aunt Bill blamed me!

That was ages ago. But Maureen is still a horrible girl, always sneering. She has grown up into a fat, white slug with a wet, sneery mouth. Aunt Bill says she might be pretty one day when she has fined down a bit. Pigs might fly, is my answer to that. And if Aunt Bill knew what Maureen says about her, she wouldn't be quite so tolerant!

Maureen is a spy. She watches from her window and when we are in the garden she lurks on the other side of the fence, listening. There is nothing wrong with being a spy, you have to be a spy if you are a child and want to know what is going on, Plato says, and he is a better spy than Maureen could ever be because he is cleverer. But he is not a mean spy, and Maureen is *mean*. She spies for mean reasons.

Aunt Bill is mad about growing things, as I've told you. One spring night, about a year ago, she woke me up to look at the cherry tree in the garden. We crept downstairs silently, because Aunt Sophie was sleeping, and out the back door.

There was a full moon and the white blossom was out and the tree was beautiful, like a pale dancer. "Oh, the darling," Aunt Bill said, and went galumphing up the garden, looking twice as large as usual in her loose cotton nightie, to fling her arms round the tree. When I reached her, she was embracing the trunk, her eyes closed, smiling blissfully, and the blossom stirred gently above her, almost as if the tree had been lonely before and was glad someone had come to love and admire it. "There, my sweet beauty," Aunt Bill murmured. She smiled at me and took my hand, and the moonlight glinted in the tears on her cheek.

"Come on in, you'll catch cold," she said. "Better not tell Sophie about this silly caper."

Aunt Sophie never knew. But someone else did. When I left for school the next day, Maureen was waiting for me. She said, "Did the moon wake you up last night? It woke me, it was full on my face. I looked out of the window and saw everything as if our gardens were floodlit."

"I keep my curtains drawn at night," I said.

But I knew that she had seen Aunt Bill and me. It was just a matter of waiting.

She said nothing all morning. She watched me from the other side of the classroom, and when she saw me looking she put her hand over her mouth and pretended to be hiding a smile. She whispered to the girl next to her and then looked at me to make sure I had noticed.

I wished I had a charm that could make me vanish. Or that she would drop dead. But neither of these useful things happened and at lunch time I was pinned against a wall in the playground by a tight mass of giggling girls. There were one or two boys of the sillier sort among them, the kind that hang around girls when there is a bit of spiteful fun to be had, but they don't count for much. If I had noticed Plato, which I hadn't, because he was sitting on the wall behind me, I would have thought he was one of them.

"You should have seen her," Maureen said. "Jane Tucker, dancing in the moonlight with her great, fat aunt . . ."

"You can't talk about *fat*, you uneducated slob," I said,

and Maureen's nasty little eyes grew even smaller and angrier.

"Oh, you think you're smart, don't you, Jane Tucker? I'll tell you something! I may not be Einstein, but at least I'm not barmy!"

"Who do you think Einstein is? A pop singer?"

She looked shifty. "He's someone who's got more brains than you, anyway. No one with any brains would prance about in their garden at night stiff stark naked."

"We weren't *naked*," I bellowed, and she grinned evilly.

Several people laughed. Someone said, "What were you wearing, then?"

"We were wearing our night things. We just went for a walk in the garden."

Howls of laughter. I said, "I don't see what's funny."

Maureen said in a conversational tone, "She lives with these potty old women. One's not so bad, just a bit scatty. The other one really is bonkers. Talks to herself all the time, my mum and I crease up laughing, other side of the fence."

"You shouldn't listen," I said. "It's bad manners. And Aunt Bill doesn't talk to herself. She talks to the plants to get them to grow. It's quite usual."

"My mum talks to her plants sometimes," a girl said. She had a timid voice. I tried to see who it was but all I could see were unfriendly, sly faces.

"Bet that's *all* she does, though!" Maureen flung this over her shoulder. Then looked at me. "Jane Tucker's fat auntie does a lot more. She makes *love* to trees, puts her arms round them and *kisses* them." She pulled her horrible mouth into a disgusted grimace. "Ugh. She's a *pervert*."

"She is not! You're perverted, up all night, spying on people. That's what perverts do. Peeping Toms . . ."

That was no good, I could see. I said, "She didn't kiss the tree, just put her arms round it." But that didn't help either. Putting your arms round a tree was enough to get you certified raving at our comprehensive. Everyone started laughing.

One girl said, "Oh, come to my bosom, my lovely oak tree," holding out her arms in a circle, closing her eyes and making vile sucking noises. And another girl started to sing a song, or a couple of lines of a song, using a dirty word to rhyme with my surname.

I was afraid I was going to cry. I knew I was going to cry.

Then someone said, "What Maureen saw was a secret religious rite. And that's a dangerous thing to see. If I were you, Maureen, I would lock my bedroom door tonight. Not that it will help much. The spirits will get you if they want to. And they *will* want to. They don't care to be spied on!"

I turned around and saw Plato for the first time. Of course, I didn't know his name then; he was just a skinny boy, sitting on the wall. He took his spectacles off and blinked.

"What religion?" Maureen said.

"The old religion. Much older than church or chapel." He had a deep impressive voice—a huge voice, for his size.

"Do you mean Druids?" That was the timid girl again, and this time I thought I saw her: a small, dark girl in the middle of the crowd. Then she vanished.

"Older than that," the skinny boy said. "It's so old that only a very few special people know about it. Aristocrats mostly. The Queen, almost certainly. A few really old families."

"Who are you kidding?" Maureen said. But she was looking uneasy.

"I'm not kidding anyone," the boy said. "I was just telling you. I felt sorry for you, carrying on like that, not knowing what you were getting into. The old religion has its Protectors, you see, and they are more sinister than Jane Tucker's aunt. Rouse them up and you'll be in dead trouble. Dark forces all round you."

He drew in a sharp, whistling breath as if *he* were nervous, and put his glasses back on. Maureen was frowning at him and I saw her throat move as she swallowed. She more than half believed him. I knew he was talking rubbish, but Maureen was addicted to horror videos, especially those with a whiff of Satan about them.

He said, shaking his head solemnly, "When you sup with the Underworld, it's as well to use a long spoon."

I laughed. Several other people laughed too, but it was me Maureen looked at. She said, "I shouldn't laugh if I were you. If that's the sort of thing your aunt is doing, I should watch out for yourself, too."

"Oh, the Devil looks after his own," the skinny boy said.

The bell rang at that moment and Maureen and her crew melted away. "Thanks," I said.

"That's okay." He hesitated before he slid off the wall. He was shorter than I was, and I guessed he was self-conscious about it. He stretched his neck and squared his shoulders. "I liked the sound of your aunt. And I hate bullies," he said.

He was waiting for me after school. I saw him outside the gate on his bike. He caught up with me as I turned the corner and scooted in the gutter beside me, standing up on the pedals to make himself taller. He said, "Hallo, Jane Tucker. My name is Plato Jones. Jones, because my father is Welsh, although he lives in America, and Plato because my mother is Greek, although she lives here. My sister's name is Aliki and she lives with our father and I live with our mother." He looked at me nervously, as if he was afraid I might laugh. If Maureen had been around I might have done, but she wasn't. So even though I was surprised to be given all this information, I just smiled encouragingly.

He looked relieved and said, "That's okay, then. Mind if I come with you?"

"It's a free country," I said.

It was several weeks before I found out that he lived in a

block of flats at the other end of the town, in quite the opposite direction.

That was the beginning. But it was summer now. The fruit had ripened on Aunt Bill's cherry tree, and the stream at the bottom of the school field had dwindled to a damp, smelly ditch. First Formers played there at lunch times, making camps in the shelter of the old willow trees, but out of school hours it was deserted, and a good place to meet; midway between us, and private.

Although I don't have a bike, I was there that afternoon before Plato. And when he did arrive, he was too winded to speak. He sat down on the bank and puffed away with his inhaler. At least it gave me a chance to tell him what had happened with my father. If he hadn't had asthma, it would have been difficult to get a word in with Plato!

"Srehtompets," he wheezed, when I had finished.

"Srehtom—oh, *stepmothers*. Give over, Plato, no one's listening."

He grinned, showing the braces on his teeth and the remains of the last meal he had eaten; green cress and white cheese by the look of it. He said hoarsely, "Seems like you've got a wicked one."

"You mean my father's wife?"

"Same thing, isn't it?"

"But she's no kind of mother. She doesn't even know me!"

"Sure of that?"

"Of course! I would have remembered!"

"Not if you were a baby at the time. Work it out, pea brain! If Annabel is ten now, and you're thirteen, then your father must have married her mother when you were about two. If he seemed to think you knew he was married, he must have had a reason for thinking that, mustn't he? It's not because he told you, because it's not the sort of thing a person of two could understand just by hearing the *words*. So you must have met your stepmother."

"Stop calling her that!" I don't know why it made me angry, but it did. I said, "Her name's Amy."

"Okay. Amy." Though his voice was still raspy, talking seemed to have deepened and oiled it. "You went to the wedding. Or he took you home. And she didn't like you."

"You only say that because your stepmother doesn't like you and you don't like her, and you want someone else to be in the same boat."

"Maybe," he said calmly. "But it seems reasonable, doesn't it? Your aunts wouldn't have adopted you if your father could have looked after you in his own family."

"I don't know." I thought, I don't *want* to know, either! I said, "If I'd lived with them, with my father and HER, then I wouldn't be *me*. I'd be someone quite different."

I felt different already. Less solid somehow. I said, "Okay. If you're right about HER, I don't mind. In fact, I'm *glad* if she didn't like me. Because if she had, I'd have missed Aunt Bill and Aunt Sophie."

"And *this* way you miss out on your brother and sister."

"They might be horrid." They hadn't *looked* horrid. I said, "I don't want to see HER, I never want to see HER. But I'd like to see them!"

Plato sucked his teeth. Making a second meal, I thought sourly. He peered over his glasses. "Why not? Find out where they live, that's the first thing."

"SHE doesn't want me to see them. I told you! And it's no good asking Aunt Bill or Aunt Sophie for their address. They'd be scared I'd write and make trouble."

"I didn't tell you to ask your aunts, did I? I said *find out*. Use your initiative!"

He was grinning away to himself. "Kids like us have to keep their ears and eyes open. Haven't I always told you?"

He had told me, over and over, and I hadn't believed him. Or, rather, I had thought that what might be true for Plato was not true for me. Plato's parents never seemed to tell him what was happening; whether he was going to America for the summer holidays, or to Greece with his mother, or to Wales to stay with his Uncle Emlyn. He had to listen on the extension when his mother was talking to his father in New York, and steam open her letters. He said, "More reliable than just asking. You can't trust grown-ups not to lie. It's their nature to keep things from kids if they can."

I had been quite sure Aunt Bill and Aunt Sophie were different, but I had been wrong, I saw now. All grown-ups were the same; all equally bad when it came to cheating on children.

Chapter Three

I gave the Aunts one more chance.

Aunt Bill was painting the thistles on the rubbish heap at the end of the garden, a lovely, fuzzy, goldeny picture that was nearly finished. Aunt Sophie stood beside her with her arms folded. I was in the bathroom. When I had pulled the plug, I stood at the open window.

Aunt Bill's voice carried clearly on the still evening air. "What gets my goat is that he left it to you to tell her. Isn't that typical? Edward all over."

"We are responsible for Jane," Aunt Sophie said. "And Edward is a sensitive man."

"Sensitive! Ha!" Aunt Bill tossed her head, like a horse. "Weak, I'd say. Can't stand up to that silly girl. Never could, from the beginning."

I wondered if she meant me but it seemed that she didn't. "Amy's young," Aunt Sophie said. "A man marries a young wife, he feels he has to indulge her."

"Not to this extent. Not to turn his back on his mother-less daughter."

"He never did that, Bill," Aunt Sophie said. "You know how he tried. It wasn't his fault."

"Nothing is ever Edward's fault, in your view," Aunt Bill said, and tossed her head again.

Aunt Bill and Aunt Sophie hardly ever quarrelled. I leaned out of the window. "Hey," I said. "*Hey!* I'm here. I'm not a tree or a plant. I've got *ears*. What's it all about?"

They both looked up and saw me. Aunt Sophie walked

down the garden and stood under the window. She said, "I thought you went to see Plato."

Her voice was reproachful. I said, "I came back."

"So I see."

She was frowning. I said sarcastically, "Do you mean I ought to shout and stamp about when I come in, just in case you're talking about me?"

She said, "Hush, dear. Of course not." I saw her glance at next door and wondered if Pig Maureen was listening. That turned me cold. I slammed down the window.

I lay with my face squashed in the pillow. Aunt Bill sat on my bed. She said, "I'm sorry, pet. My poor pettikins."

She stroked my hair and I jerked away. "Don't *pity* me," I said. "I'm not a baby. I've got all my mental faculties. I just want to *know*."

"Sophie said she did her best to explain."

I said, through gritted teeth, "SHE doesn't want me to see my own brother and sister. So you don't want me to see them, either. Why not? Are you afraid of HER? Does she hate me? How can she hate me if she doesn't know me?"

I swivelled round on the pillow and reared up a bit. I could see my red face in the mirror, screwed up and blotchy. My hair looked nice, though; sun-streaked brown, thick and shiny. I sat up properly and combed it with my fingers and shook it round my shoulders. Aunt Bill watched me with a sad expression. I wished I could squeeze out a few tears, but my eyes were quite dry. I put my head on one side and made my voice shake a bit. "I honestly don't understand."

"Then don't try. It's not worth it," Aunt Bill said, still looking sad but sounding much brisker. "It's nothing but silliness. Ordinary human silliness. Nothing more."

And I knew that was all she was going to tell me.

Plato's mother answered when I rang Sunday morning. She said in her waily voice—waily, partly because she is

foreign, but mostly because she is that sort of person—
"Oh, Jane, I cannot disturb Plato while he is doing his homework."

That was rubbish, of course. Plato could do the soppy kid's homework they are given in his class in a blindfold and strait-jacket and still hold six separate conversations and play a game of chess on the side. The fact was, Mrs Jones couldn't bear anyone to divert his attention from her at weekends; she would keep him away from school during the week and make him play Scrabble with her all day, if it wasn't against the law.

I said brightly, "That's all right, Mrs Jones, I quite understand, and it doesn't matter. I'm going to a gig with Aunt Sophie and we'll be passing your block, so I can easily drop a note in for him."

I wrote, DIER PLETU, NU LACK ET HUMI. BIGON UPIRETOUN TACKIR.

A simple vowel substitution code was quite complicated enough to fool Mrs Jones. I didn't put LUVI JENI all the same. Even someone whose brain had been softened with television soaps could crack that!

I put the letter in an envelope and wrote PLATO JONES VERY PRIVATE AND PERSONAL in huge letters. Then I stuck just the tip of the flap down very lightly so that Mrs Jones could open it easily. I had no evidence that she was given to spying, like Plato, but it seemed wise to make sure.

Aunt Sophie and Aunt Bill sat in the front seats and I got in the back with the drums. I had to sit with my knees jammed against my ears, and when we got to Plato's block I could barely move. This gave me a good idea. I crept up the path to the front entrance with my right leg collapsing beneath me, shoved the letter through the slit, pressed the Jones's buzzer, and limped back to the car. "You all right, pet?" Aunt Bill asked, observing my crab-like approach.

"Fine," I said, with a grave, martyred smile. "Just a tummy ache. I expect it'll go off in a minute."

I made to open the rear door, and winced. "I don't want to miss the gig," I gasped. "But I don't want to hold you up, either. It's only one of my cramps. It always gets better if I walk for a bit."

I knew the Aunts were too polite to question me about this. Aunt Sophie looked thoughtful, as if she were checking out a few dates in her head, but Aunt Bill was simply concerned. "You all right to walk home alone? Want me to come with you?"

I shook my head gallantly, backing away from the car, waving and grinning. Aunt Bill poked her head through the window and shouted the usual instructions about going straight home and being careful crossing the main road. I stuck my thumbs in my ears and waggled my fingers to show that these boring messages had been received and understood, and she smote her chest with her fist and rolled her eyes, miming her apology for being so fussy.

As soon as Rattlebones had clattered round the corner, I straightened up and sped home. Aunt Sophie had drawn the blinds against the sun and the light inside the house was watery green. I saw myself in the long hall mirror and thought I looked like a mermaid under the water. I swam with my arms and swayed my hips, keeping my legs pressed together to make a tail.

I was embarrassed about what I was going to do. Since I had been old enough to put my own clothes away, neither Aunt Bill nor Aunt Sophie had opened my cupboards or drawers. I had never needed to worry about leaving a diary or a notebook lying about; they would never look at something private, not even a holiday postcard that was not addressed to them! They would be horrified to think I might behave differently.

Aunt Sophie's desk was in the music room. It was very neat. Each drawer was labelled—HOUSEHOLD EXPENSES, INSURANCE, GIGS, CAR DOCU-

MENTS—and as far as I could tell had the right papers inside. There was a drawer labelled EQUIPMENT that had boxes of staples and rolls of sticky tape and packets of pens. And one labelled PERSONAL that was locked.

That surprised me to start with. Then shocked me. No one locked drawers—or doors, except the bathroom door—in our house.

I knew what was in the drawer because I had often seen it open when Aunt Sophie was busy at her desk. She kept letters from friends there, birthday cards that people had sent her, a brown envelope that had a piece of my baby hair inside tied with red ribbon, and my mother's wedding ring in a flat velvet box, which she was keeping for me when I was older. What else? What was it she didn't want me see? She would never lock the drawer against Aunt Bill. She trusted Aunt Bill.

I felt my face growing hot. Well, she was right not to trust *me*, it seemed. And yet, as I thought about it, the fact that she *had* locked the drawer made me feel less ashamed. Since she didn't trust me, there was no need for me to feel bad about behaving like someone who wasn't trustworthy.

The more I thought about it, the more indignant I felt. I had never before looked through Aunt Sophie's private things and she should have known that. How horrible of her to lock her drawer as if I were that sort of prying person. That I was prying now was nothing to do with it: she had *thought* about it before I had *done* it!

I wished I could pick the lock. Plato had told me that he knew how to open locks with one of his mother's credit cards, but Aunt Bill and Aunt Sophie refused to use what they called 'plastic money'. Except for the bills that came through the post, like gas and electricity, they paid cash for everything.

Besides, if I had had a credit card I wouldn't have known how to pick a lock with it. My education in that sort of skill has been severely neglected.

I rattled the drawer a few times but it wouldn't budge. I thought the top of the desk looked somehow different. Emptier. Something missing. The telephone was there, and the blotter, and some sheets of music with Aunt Sophie's latest composition half-finished, and her beautiful glass paper weight that had a waterlily pattern inside it, and the wooden foot roller that she used to massage her feet when she had been standing a long time and drumming, and the red leather diary I had given her as part of last year's Christmas present.

Of course, that was it! The diary was there, but not the matching address book. When I wrote to my father, I sent the letter to the ship, but if he had a wife and children then he must have a house or a flat . . .

And Aunt Sophie had guessed I would want to know where!

I chuckled as I went upstairs. "Start by assuming he lives in London until we've proved otherwise," Plato had said. "Near the London docks, not too far from Southampton. Lots of big ships used to dock at Tilbury, some cruise ships still do. Plenty of sailors living in the East End of London. Missions to seamen."

Aunt Bill's room is always higgledy-piggledy and smelling of turpentine. The thistle picture was on the easel and I thought it was lovely; yellow and glowing as if there were a light behind it. (I wish I could paint like Aunt Bill, or compose, like Aunt Sophie, but I am hopeless at music and art. All I can do is write stories.)

In Aunt Bill's drawers, socks and underwear and sweaters were all tangled together. I tugged at the toe of a pair of green tights and most of the things in the drawer came tumbling out, clothes and papers meshed up like a huge, untidy bird's nest. Right at the bottom there was a postcard of Brighton from me, sent years and years ago one summer Aunt Sophie and I had gone to the sea on our own. It was written in pencil, in joined-up letters, but before I

30

could spell. 'Deer Rnt Bill, I am hevin a nic tim. I hope you r well.'

I thought it was sweet of Aunt Bill to have kept this juvenile effort, although there was nothing else in her drawers to remind her of me; no other postcards or letters, not even a photograph. This surprised me for a minute because Aunt Bill never threw anything out in the ordinary way. Then I remembered that every now and again, when Aunt Sophie went on a cleaning binge, Aunt Bill would heave a lot of stuff into a cardboard box and carry it up to the attic.

"Out of sight, out of mind," she would say, because Aunt Sophie hasn't been up to the attic for years, not since the time she found a family of bats living there. "Dear little creatures," Aunt Bill called them, but Aunt Sophie was terrified they would fly at her and get trapped in her hair.

Where bats are concerned—and mice, and spiders, and snakes—I come midway between Aunt Bill and Aunt Sophie. I am not frightened, but I can live without them quite happily. So I was relieved, on the whole, when I creaked open the door of the attic and nothing scurried or fluttered. It was very peaceful; dusty light shafting in through the dormer window, and the only sound a soft ticking from the water tank in the corner. There was a dressmaker's dummy that had belonged to Aunt Sophie's mother. Otherwise, everything in this little room under the rafters belonged to Aunt Bill: suitcases with broken catches, old picture frames, stacks of canvases, a trunk labelled OLD CLOTHES USEFUL FOR GARDENING and, of course, lots of brimming full cardboard boxes.

There were boxes of Aunt Bill's old shoes—running shoes gone at the toes, and leather sandals that had lost straps or buckles. There was a box with a dead-looking fur squashed into it, a coat someone had given Aunt Bill that she wouldn't wear because of cruelty to animals, but had thought it unkind to refuse; several boxes of coloured pebbles from the sea shore, and others with cracked jugs and plates that she sometimes used when she was painting a still life. The rest were full of a jumble of rubbish; bits of string, half-used packets of gardening labels, and dried-up tubes of paint, as if she had emptied out an untidy drawer in a hurry when Aunt Sophie was on the war path. There were photographs, too; some old and yellowing, some still in the envelopes as they had come from the chemist.

"Look for clues," Plato had said. "Clues to your past."

I wasn't sure I would know a clue when I saw it. But I had plenty of time. I sat on the floor, emptied the boxes around me, and looked through the things carefully, sorting them out a bit as I put them back because, although I am nowhere as neat as Aunt Sophie, I don't care for muddle.

I had seen most of the photographs before. The most interesting ones were pictures of Aunt Bill and Aunt Sophie when they were babies held by their mothers—the twin sisters who were exactly alike—and of their two fathers, who were not alike at all. Aunt Bill's father was a huge man with short arms, a bit like a bear. Aunt Sophie's father was wispy and delicate. There were pictures of the Aunts as little girls, years ago in the war, with the fathers in uniform and the mothers in hats, and pictures of them paddling at the seaside with their dresses tucked in their knickers. The only pictures of me were discards. Either the light had got in, or I had moved out of focus. Aunt Bill, who had taken them, had stuck all the good ones into the album that was kept with the World Atlas and the *Encyclopedia Britannica* and other tall books on the bottom shelf of the bookcase in the sitting room.

And that was where I found the first clue to my past. Not locked away, not hidden at all, but where it had always been, where I could always have found it if I had known where to look. Or known there was something to look for.

★

Aunt Bill had always taken a picture of me on my birthday, which is the second of May, beside the cherry tree that was planted the year I was born and has grown up with me. Whenever we looked at these pictures, she always remarked on the tree, how much faster it grew than a human child, and I suppose that had stopped me from seeing the clue that had been under my nose all the time.

Even now I didn't see it immediately. I was just flipping over the pages. My first birthday, my second birthday, my fourth birthday, my fifth birthday (wearing my new school clothes and carrying a new satchel), my sixth birthday (with a gap between my front teeth), my seventh birthday . . .

It was only then that I realised. I turned back to check. My third birthday was missing.

Chapter Four

Although I rang and rang, Plato's number was always busy, and so I had plenty of time to work out what to say in Backspeak. When I finally got him, I said it, "On emit klat ni edoc," and heard him giggle.

He said. "That's okay, she can't hear. But I've got no time for games, either. I'm trying to work through the phone book while she's in the bath. There are hundreds of Tuckers. Nineteen E. Tuckers. Does he have another initial?"

"I don't know." I felt silly, admitting this. I said, "I can ask the Aunts when they come back from the gig."

"Give me patience!" he said, "You don't need to *ask*. Look for your birth certificate, dopey! That might give us a clue about where he lives, too. It would say where he lived when you were born, anyway. He might not have moved. Or not far away. Hang about—I think I can hear the bath water." He lowered his voice and said, putting on a Welsh accent, "This is Jones the Spy signing off. Over and out."

Typical Plato! So keen to say what he had been up to that he left no space for me to say what I had found out. Just as talking in code was only a "game" when *he* was too busy to play it. Or too busy playing his own game. Jones the Spy. That was because in the Welsh valley his father came from there were so many people called Jones that they had to be set apart from one another. The postman was Jones the

34

Post, the fishmonger, Jones the Fish, and Plato's Uncle Emlyn, who was a teacher, was Jones the School.

I was fed up with myself as well as with Plato. *I* should have thought of my birth certificate. The stupid thing was, I had seen it last year when Aunt Sophie had sent off for my passport before I went to France on the school camping holiday. But I hadn't looked at it properly. I hadn't been interested. I wasn't suspicious, like Plato. I hadn't needed to be, until now.

My passport was in my room, but Aunt Sophie had kept the birth certificate. Since I hadn't seen it when I went through her desk, it had to be in the PERSONAL drawer. Which was locked.

I looked at my passport. Beside *Place of Birth*, it said *London*. As soon as I saw this, it seemed that I had known it all along, and I could have kicked myself for not remembering it earlier. I must be such a dim, unnoticing person! Plato would be right to despise me! Though he would be glad to know he was on the right track, wading through the London telephone directory.

I rattled the knob of the PERSONAL drawer but it wouldn't budge. I pulled out the drawer above. There was a piece of board beneath it, covering the locked drawer, but there was a gap at the back and my hand was small enough to slip through. I could feel the edge of a plastic folder and the edge of an envelope. The folder was too wide and too stiff to come through the gap but the envelope was softer and narrower, and although I scraped my knuckles quite badly, I managed to wriggle it out without tearing it.

It was a plain brown envelope marked MARGARET'S PAPERS.

Margaret was my mother. Margaret Alisoun Tucker. I had always thought it odd that my father had not given me one of her names to remember her by. Perhaps he had thought it would be unlucky, when she had died so sadly, so young.

Her birth certificate was there, her marriage certificate, and her death certificate. There was nothing wrong in my seeing these things, but because I was snooping I felt uncomfortable and only glanced at them quickly. Her driving licence was there, and a couple of library tickets, and a piece of paper that said she had passed her bronze life-saving medal. I thought this was an odd assortment of things and I wondered who had put them into the envelope; the writing on it wasn't my father's and it wasn't Aunt Sophie's. I shook the envelope and several more tickets fell out—green ones and white ones, like tickets from the cleaner or the shoe repairer—and, last of all, my birth certificate, folded up small. When I opened it, I saw that it had been torn into quarters and then mended with sticky tape. I wondered who had done that and why, and then I remembered that the certificate Aunt Sophie had sent to the passport office last year had not looked like this one, patched and grubby, but clean and new with the words typed instead of handwritten.

This certificate must be the original one and the other a copy. Perhaps Aunt Sophie had thought the old one too messy. Or perhaps she hadn't been able to find it. I thought that the court must have wanted my birth certificate when I was adopted, so it was possible that Aunt Sophie had been to Somerset House where the records are kept and had the copy made then.

Either way, this battered old birth certificate was clearly mine. Jane, plain Jane, no second name, born on the second of May. Mother, Margaret Alisoun Tucker. Father, Horatio Edward Tucker. All of 44, Shipshape Street, in the Metropolitan District of Bow.

I don't know how I lived through the rest of that day. I was desperate to tell Plato. I didn't dare ring him. His mother would be out of the bath by now and draped on the sofa with her cigarettes and gin at the ready, in preparation for a delirious evening of Scrabble. (If this sounds as if I didn't have much patience with Plato's mother at this time, then it sounds right!)

Besides, Aunt Bill and Aunt Sophie came home about half an hour later. And because they were tired, Aunt Sophie from drumming, and Aunt Bill from wearing shoes and not being able to finish her thistle picture, I had to get supper for all of us. Not that I minded.

I meant to creep downstairs after the Aunts were in bed and look through the telephone directory for Horatio Tuckers, but although I thought I could keep myself awake by reciting long poems in Backspeak, I hardly got beyond *Ts Senga Eve, ha rettib llihc ti saw*, before I found myself drifting away under the soft featheriness of the duvet.

When I woke, it was morning and later than usual. Too late to walk to school, so Aunt Bill had to drive me in Rattle-bones. (The school where Aunt Sophie taught the piano was in a different direction, and, anyway, she usually went on her bike.)

I said, "You know that album you did of me, all my birthday pictures? I was looking at it yesterday and there isn't one of me when I was three. Was it raining?"

"Can't remember." She didn't sound very interested.

I said, "I never noticed before. I suppose I spent longer looking because I was left on my own and wanted something quiet to do." I thought that might make her feel guilty. In case it didn't, I added pathetically, "I wasn't feeling very well."

"All right now, aren't you?"

"Mmm. I just wondered . . ."

She said nothing. Perhaps she hadn't heard me. Except when Rattlebones was resting in a traffic jam, or at a red light, this conversation was conducted at the top of our voices.

I said, "I only mean, it seems odd. There's one of me at two, and one of me at four, and one of me . . ."

"I stuck them in the album. I do remember."

"I thought you would. I said to myself, *Aunt Bill always remembers.*"

"Kind of you." She glanced at me with half of a smile. Then she said, "It's not a big secret. You spent your third birthday with your father and Amy. When they got married, he thought, they both thought, you should live with them. There was nothing we could say. It seemed natural and sensible. But it turned out you were too young to transplant. You came back to us. Came home. And that was the end of it. All's well that ends well."

I said, "I'm glad I came back. But why didn't Amy like me? What did I do wrong?"

"Who said anything about doing *wrong*? Heavens above, you were only a baby. No one could blame you!"

"*Did* anyone blame me?"

"No. No, of course not." But the veins in her cheek had suddenly reddened.

She stopped outside the school and said firmly and almost crossly, "Don't make a meal of it, poppet. Maybe it would have been better if we'd told you before. But it never seemed the right moment. Hard to know what to say to a child about adult foolishness. Your father loves Amy, but that's not to deny she's a difficult woman. And I daresay Sophie and I were difficult too, and made things harder for her than we need have done. But we'd had the care of you since you were a few days old. We couldn't just hand you over, wave goodbye, and wash our hands of you. We loved you too much. And of course Amy thought we criticised her all the time. A couple of interfering old maids. Nutty as fruit cakes. Ha!" She gave a loud, indignant snort. "Your father was caught in the crossfire. Ducking for cover as usual!"

This was all quite interesting, but not what I wanted to

know. I didn't care how they had all felt. It was a long time ago and nothing to do with me anymore. I wanted to know about Annabel and George but there was no point in asking Aunt Bill. She was only interested in the grown-ups, not in the children. I would be wasting my breath.

Chapter Five

"I expect it was Amy who tore up your birth certificate," Plato said. "Then thought she'd gone too far and stuck it together again. I bet my stepmother would like to tear me up sometimes!"

I thought that Plato must be a discouraging stepson. Always watching and judging.

I said, "Stepmothers are not always awful. Only in books."

"And in my experience, too," Plato said. Then he looked a little shame-faced. "That's not fair! My experience is limited to one, and she's no worse than my mother and father. In fact she's a whole lot better in some ways. She doesn't smoke or knock back the gin, and even if she doesn't like me very much, I can't really say that's a black mark against her. And she likes Aliki and Aliki likes her. Aliki was coming to England this summer. But there was a letter for my mother this morning. Aliki wants to stay in the States for the holidays and go with THEM to a house on a lake. They asked me to come, but I can't, of course." He pulled a sour face and sighed. "Someone has to look out for my mother."

"Is she very upset about Aliki?"

"She will be, soon as she opens the letter. I shoved it at the bottom of the pile once I'd gummed it up again, but she'll have read it by now."

It was after school. Plato had been riding me around on his cross bar, looking for a telephone box that was working and had a directory in it. We had found one outside the post office and were waiting for the fat lady inside to finish her conversation. I said, "Perhaps she'll be over the worst by the time you get home."

"You're hopeful," Plato said. He looked tired, but perhaps it was only his asthma; it must have been an effort, pedalling my weight on his bike. He was wheezing a bit; his voice sounded dusty. He said, "I'm fed up, too. I was looking forward to seeing Aliki."

I felt ashamed because I was glad that she wasn't coming. I said, "You'll have me. We might go to Dorset to stay with some friends for a week, but that's all. But I suppose I'm not as good as a sister!"

"Just as *good*. Just not the *same*. She's younger than me. I have to look after her. So it's different from a friend. I mean, I have to *worry* about her."

I thought, I would probably worry about Annabel and George if I knew them. Only I didn't. I hadn't been allowed to. I said, crossly, "I wouldn't know about that. It sounds soppy to me."

"Yako," Plato said.

"What do you mean? Okay what?"

"Yako, stel og."

He got on his bike.

I said, "Let's go where?"

The fat lady had finished her call and was backing out of the telephone box, laden with shopping bags, pushing the door with her big bottom. "Sorry to keep you waiting," she said. She beamed at us. "I'm always like that when I get on to my sister!"

"That's all right," Plato said, smiling back. Then, to me, "Let's go anywhere. Home, if you like. No point in hanging round here if you think being interested in your brother and sister is soppy."

"Don't be a pig."

"Is that what I am? I know that I snort and snuffle, though

41

it's not polite to rub it in, is it? But I wasn't aware that I walked on four legs. And you'd have to fatten me up quite a lot to make me worth killing for bacon."

He giggled at his own brilliant wit. I felt murderous.

I said, "If you go on like that, I'll kill you just for the thrill of it. I'm not surprised your stepmother doesn't like you if you make stupid jokes all the time . . . Oh, *please*, Plato! It's not fair! You know I can't do it without you. If we got the right number, it would be awful if I'd made the call. My father might answer!"

"So? No reason why you shouldn't ring him up, is there?"

The idea made me feel sick. And so cold that I actually started to shiver. How I felt must have shown in my face because he got off his bike at once. He said, "You're right, I'm a pig. A foul pig. Though I believe if pigs are given the chance to keep clean, they're quite fastidious animals." He opened the door of the telephone box.

I said, "Don't tease me, Plato!"

"Okay. I'm sorry." He took his glasses off to read the directory and he looked different without them. Naked, and younger. He frowned, and muttered under his breath, "Tucker, F. Tucker, F. E. Tucker, Frederick. Tucker, G. Tucker, Georgina. Tucker, G. W. Family Butcher. Tucker, H. Tucker, H. A. . . . ."

I said, "Stop, Plato. I feel *faint*. My head's swimmy and my hands have gone sticky."

"Girls!" he said. "Sit down and put your head between your knees. Do you want me to stop?"

He peered blindly at me. I shook my head.

"Tucker, H. E. is Oakwood Avenue, SW14, which is somewhere like Barnes, I think. Tucker, Harold . . ." He let out a triumphant crow. "Hang on, Jane. We've got him. Tucker, Horatio . . ."

I hung on to the door of the telephone box. I couldn't speak.

42

"Shipshape Street, E3," Plato said. "But not 44, I'm afraid. Number 22. Looks as if he moved up the road. It may not be him, of course."

He put his glasses back on and blinked at me. Although he smiled, I knew he was almost as scared as I was. He took his inhaler out of his pocket, looked at it, and put it back. Then he took out the phone card that his mother insisted he carry with him in case he should have an accident and need to ring home. He said, "Shall I?"

"Suppose they guess?"

"They won't. I meant, do you want me to? *Really?*"

"I think so."

"Can't do any harm," he said thoughtfully—as if he were persuading himself rather than me. He took his inhaler out again and this time he used it. Then he punched the buttons. I could hear the number ringing. Ringing and ringing. I thought that they must be out and felt weak with relief. Then someone answered. Plato looked at me and winked. He said, using the deep voice he always seemed able to produce when he wanted, "Good afternoon. Is that Mrs Tucker? Do you have a few moments to answer one or two questions? This is a government survey."

I could hear a female voice quacking briefly, though not what she said.

"Education," Plato said. "It won't take long, Mrs Tucker. I am a civil servant working in the Ministry of Education. Would you be so good as to tell me how many children you have, and their ages?" He paused, the female voice quacked. "A boy and a girl," Plato said. "And the girl is the older. Thank you, Mrs Tucker. Now, if I may know your husband's occupation?" More quacking. "A marine engineer," Plato said. "A mariner. That must mean a fairly lonely life for you, Mrs Tucker. Still, the children keep you company, I suppose. Now all I need is the name of the school they attend at the moment." He listened. "Shipshape Primary, thank you, Mrs Tucker. That is the name of your street, so I assume it must be conveniently near. Convenience is one of the matters we are covering in our survey. Thank you, Mrs Tucker. You have been most helpful. My name, should you wish to check my credentials, is Theodore Roosevelt. Like the famous American President. Thank you again. And good day to you."

He put the telephone down and looked at me. He had sounded so solemnly grown-up. Now he was just a little boy who had played a joke on someone, spreading his hand across his mouth and sniggering through his fingers.

I said, "That was *wonderful*. I could never have done it!"

"I got in some practice last night. I started off pretending I was doing research for a drug company, asking how many people there were in the family and what sort of medicines they took, but that didn't work so well. People don't like to tell you they take laxatives or stomach pills. And the people who didn't mind sounded old. Too old to have children. So I thought about education. It seemed the obvious thing."

I thought it was bad for him to be so pleased with himself. I said, "Why didn't you ask HER what she did for a job? It's old-fashioned to think it's only husbands go out to work."

"Sexist, you mean. I did think of that. But then I thought, since they must realise I know their address, they might think I was a burglar trying to find out if they were out in the day."

"You didn't sound like a burglar. You sounded respectable."

"Some burglars must sound respectable. I just didn't want anyone to start worrying after they'd put the phone down. People don't worry about education."

I said, "What did SHE sound like?"

"Quite nice. Quite young. A bit proud."

"How do you mean?"

"As if she was putting on her best manners in case I was

44

someone important. But if she'd decided I wasn't, she might have turned haughty. Why don't you ring yourself, if you're curious?"

I found myself trembling. "I couldn't!"

"You don't have to say who you are. You can pretend you've got a wrong number."

"It might not be *them.*"

"Then it wouldn't matter, would it? Ask for Elizabeth Tucker. Say, is that Elizabeth Tucker? She might say, no, this is Amy. Then we'd be certain we'd got the right people."

"There can't be two Horatio Tuckers who live in Ship-shape Street with a wife and two children!"

"Why sound so gloomy? Didn't you want to find them?"

A man said, "You children quite finished?"

He had a pink, shiny face like a satin cushion with a pinched button mouth in the middle. He said, "Telephone boxes are not places to play in, you know."

"I'm sorry, Sir," Plato said. He stood aside and held the door open. "Though we weren't *playing.* My poor grandmother has just fallen downstairs and broken both her legs and her collar bone, and my father has sent me to ring my uncles and aunts. We've got a telephone at home but it's been cut off because my father lost his job last month and we haven't paid the bill."

The man was looking startled. He said, "Well, in that case . . ."

"Oh, no, Sir," Plato said. "Please make your call. I'm sure it's important. And as one of my uncles is out, I have to wait and try again in a minute. So if you won't be too long . . ." He sighed and shook his head sorrowfully. "My grandmother is ninety-seven. The doctors don't hold out much hope. And of course she would like to see her children before . . ."

The man said hastily, "Very natural. I won't hold up your errand of mercy too long."

45

He went into the telephone box and closed the door behind him. I said, "He didn't believe you."

"Not altogether," Plato said. "But he can't be sure, can he?"

He stood where the man could see him and looked anxious and solemn.

I tried to make him laugh. I said, "I'm sorry about your grandmother. Did she fall or was she pushed?"

"It's terrible to make jokes about a poor dying woman," Plato said. And then, with no change of tone or expression, "We've got a couple of days off next week. All the lower forms, while the Upper School are doing exams. Primary schools aren't on holiday. We could hang around Shipshape Street and check on the kids going home."

"How far away is it?"

"Other side of the city. I looked in the A to Z. We'd have to go up to Waterloo on the train and then on the Underground."

I said, "I'm not allowed to go to London on my own."

"You wouldn't be alone. You'd be with me. And you don't have to tell your aunts anyway. Just go off as if you were going to school."

"They'll know that I'm not! We always get a note to take home when we have a free day."

Plato looked at me pityingly. "Whatever for? I never give notes to my mother. It's the only way I ever get any time to myself."

I felt dreadfully stupid. It had never occurred to me to hide anything from Aunt Bill and Aunt Sophie even though they were stricter about where I went and what time I came home than most parents. Plato was younger than I was. But in some ways he seemed a lot older. "I suppose . . ." I began.

"Kool das," Plato hissed. He hung his head and looked even more dejected.

The man came out of the booth. He said, "All yours now.

I hope you have better news of your grandmother when you get home."

Plato smiled bravely. "Thank you, Sir." He kept his head down while the man walked away. Then he grinned at me. "You going to ring?"

"Yako," I said.

It was like the moment in a flying dream just before you fall over the edge of the cliff. The telephone rang and rang. Plato whispered, "She took a long time to answer me, too. Perhaps they're all in the garden."

Playing with the children, I thought. Perhaps my father was pushing Annabel on the swing. Or teaching George to ride his bicycle. In my mind I saw them in tall, flowery grass, running and laughing.

The telephone rang. And rang. Then someone picked it up and my stomach turned over.

"Hallo," my father said.

I didn't answer. I couldn't speak. I was frozen.

"Ted Tucker here," my father said. "Who is it?"

Another voice joined in. A little, high voice. "Hallo. Hallo."

"Put the phone down, George darling," my father said.

"I want to speak, Daddy. I want to speak on the telephone."

My father laughed. "Hallo, George. Goodbye, George."

"I don't want to speak to you, Daddy. I want to speak to the people."

I thought, he is on an extension! If my father puts his receiver down, I could say, "Hallo, George."

But my father laughed again. He said, "It's all right, Georgie. You can put the phone down. There isn't anyone to speak to. There isn't anyone there."

Chapter Six

I ate school dinners but Plato took a packed lunch because his mother was afraid of germs in the school kitchen. I could have got up early and taken something from the fridge, but I felt bad enough letting Aunt Bill and Aunt Sophie think I was going to school just as usual, without cheating in that way as well. Besides, I knew that Plato, who packed his own lunches because his mother was always too tired to get up in the mornings, would have plenty for both of us.

We ate several smoked salmon sandwiches in the train to Waterloo. I had eaten smoked salmon only once or twice in my life, as a treat, but Plato said that his mother bought it every week. "You don't have to cook it. She says there's no point in cooking just for the two of us. I get bored with it sometimes."

I thought I could live on smoked salmon for ever and ever, but I didn't say so. It seemed to make Aunt Bill and Aunt Sophie sound either poor or mean to say that we couldn't afford it. I said, "Aunt Sophie says too much smoked stuff gives you allergies. Perhaps it's what causes your asthma."

"It's supposed to be something in the air," he said. "Dust or pollen. That's why it's worse in the summer."

He stared at me, his mouth slightly open and his eyelids drooping; a stupid expression he often wore when he was thinking. Then he said, "Still, maybe you're right. You'd better eat the rest of the sandwiches and I'll make out with the peaches and the chocolate chip cookies."

I didn't care about the peaches, but I love chocolate chip cookies. In fact, along with mashed banana with sugar and cream, they are my favourite things in this world. Plato knew this because I had told him. He also knew that I wasn't allowed many sweet things at home. I said, "Chocolate ruins your teeth," and he smiled, very sweetly.

"Well, if you eat the sandwiches and I eat the cookies, we'll be saving my lungs and your teeth."

I said, "I suppose if you're weedy and small you have to be sharp. But you'll cut yourself one day." And I gazed out of the window at the allotments on the railway embankment and the tight-packed little houses rattling by.

"Geb nodrap," he said humbly. "You can have all the cookies. Yako?"

"Backspeak is babyish," I said. "I'm giving it up."

I sat very stiff until we got to Waterloo. Then, as the train drew in under the high glass roof, I looked at him. He was hunched up, blinking sadly behind his glasses, and I was sorry. I said, "Thank you for coming. I wouldn't have dared go without you."

He squared his shoulders. He might be easy to squash but he was quick to recover. He said, "I've worked it out on the A to Z. We can go by bus or by Underground. Bus would be more interesting but the Underground's quicker. We get off at Bow and walk through Bow Cemetery. Shipshape Street's on the other side. Bow Cemetery looks huge on the map. I wonder if it's one of the big cemeteries that were dug outside the city after the Great Plague of London. Do you know about the Great Plague? They used to put a red cross on the houses where people were dying, and write *Lord have mercy upon us*. And they trundled carts through the streets at night and shouted, *Bring out your dead*." His eyes shone with excitement.

I stuck my fingers in my ears, pretending to be shocked. "Pots ti," I said. "*Please* Otalp."

★

Even if Plato was wrong and it didn't go back to the Great Plague of London, it was still a very old cemetery. Near the main gate there were some new graves covered with granite chippings and wilting flowers, but most of the cemetery was rough, tangled wilderness, where the old trees, laurel and holly and yew, were choked with creeping ivy and the ground was dense with scrubby bushes and thick clumps of nettles. Off the main paths, the tracks were narrow and muddy; the old tombstones had fallen over, or leaned drunkenly sideways. We explored for a while, and then sat on a bench in a big grassy clearing at the side of the railway line, and shared the rest of Plato's lunch. In the end, I ate all the cookies. Plato said he had brought them for me and he didn't much like them. Except for an old woman muttering on one of the benches and an old man walking his dog, there was no one about.

We got to the school as the bell rang at the end of the morning, and stood by the railings. It was an old-fashioned school building with tall, pointed windows and steps leading up to the separate entrances for GIRLS, BOYS, and INFANTS, and a concrete playground with goal posts for netball. Children ran about, yelling. Plato said, "Will you recognise them?"

I felt very odd; both longing to see them and hoping I wouldn't. I said, "Perhaps they're not at school today. They might be having a holiday if my father's at home. Though sometimes he only gets a few days between cruises." I hoped he was safely back on his ship. I hadn't thought until now how awful it would be if he saw me. I felt my face burning.

I wanted to run. I said, "Oh, Plato, I *can't*. Let's go home."

"After we've come all this way? Don't be silly. You're not doing anything *wrong*. It's not wrong to want to see your brother and sister. It can't hurt anyone. Not just looking."

"It feels wrong, that's all."

"Are you scared they'll recognise *you*?"

I shook my head. I was too full to speak. I couldn't have run if I'd tried. I felt like a criminal.

Then I saw Annabel and I stopped being frightened at once. She was walking across the playground towards the entrance marked INFANTS. She looked just as she had done in the photograph on my father's desk: long, soft, curly hair bouncing on her shoulders. And she had the same little worried half-smile as she turned for an instant and glanced in our direction. As if she were looking for someone.

"That's her," I said. "The one in the red dress with the pretty hair."

"Don't shout!" Plato said. "She's looking at us. Do you want her to hear you?"

It was Plato who was nervous now! "I'm not shouting," I said. "And she's not looking at *us*."

She had been looking for George. He came tumbling down the steps with a lot of other small boys in jeans and green sweaters, laughing and squealing, bursting with just-out-of-school energy. His big satchel banged against his legs, pulling him sideways, and his fat cheeks were hard and rosy as apples as he ran towards Annabel.

She took his hand, bending over him, straightening his sweater under the satchel strap, and he looked up at her, laughing. They walked together across the playground, towards us. My brother and sister.

They were strangers to me, but I felt as if I had known them all my life.

Plato whispered, "Perhaps they go home for lunch."

They came out of the gate. George was chattering. "We did joined-up writing this morning. Miss Povey said I was very good, better nor anyone, but then my fingers got tired and I lost a mark at the end."

They passed so close that I could have touched them. Annabel had a green plastic bow in her hair that pulled it away from her forehead, and she was fiddling with it as if it annoyed her. I thought she might have been made to wear it at school to keep her curls off her face and it seemed I was right, because she took it off and shook her hair free and combed the curls loose with her fingers . . .

With her three fingers. She had no forefinger and no thumb, just a small, pink lump where they should have been.

I only saw this hand for an instant. She put it—and the bow—either into a pocket, or into a fold of her dress. Her other hand was holding George's. Their clasped hands swung between them. He said, "Oh, my satchel's too *heavy*," in a sudden, babyish wail and she let him go, took it from him and hung it over her own shoulder, then reached for him again, doing all this with one hand—with her right hand, her *good* hand with four fingers and thumb—and keeping her damaged hand hidden.

There was a small road at the side of the school. The rest of Shipshape Street lay beyond it; a short street of terraced houses with the green of the cemetery at the far end. Annabel and George stopped at the small road, and I was glad to see that they had been taught their road drill. They both looked left, and then right, and then left again, even though there were no cars in sight. Then they crossed as they should, neither dawdling nor running, just walking briskly. As soon as they reached the opposite side, Annabel let go George's hand and he darted ahead, jumping cracked paving stones as I had done at his age. Plato and I followed slowly.

I said, "They oughtn't to walk home alone. Someone ought to meet them."

I felt angry with their mother. Annabel was only ten years old and I had been eleven before Aunt Bill and Aunt Sophie had stopped meeting me after school.

"They haven't far to go," Plato said. "And someone's looking out for them, anyway."

The 'someone' was standing at a gate, waving. A lady in a bright yellow blouse. George ran up to her, thudding into her, and she gasped and then laughed, putting her arms round him and swinging him off the ground. She put him down and bent to kiss Annabel. She said, "Have you had a good morning, my darlings?"

She had pretty, crinkly grey hair, and a pink and white wrinkled face with a bit of a moustache on her upper lip. I wanted to stop but I thought that might seem suspicious so I marched firmly on, Plato beside me, sneaking a look at the house as we passed. It said 22 in the coloured glass of the fanlight. There were looped net curtains at all the windows, and a hanging basket of red geraniums over the porch.

Annabel and George ran up the paved path and into the open front door. The lady in the yellow blouse was still at the gate, fastening it with a loop of wire. She looked at us. And I recognised her.

I held my breath and looked back at her without blinking. For a second I thought she looked puzzled, but I could have been wrong because although she smiled, it was only in the way people smile at kids in the street.

Seeing them and not seeing them at the same time.

When we heard the front door close, we bolted. We ran to the end of the street and squeezed through a place where the railings were bent wide enough to let us through, into the cemetery.

We ran along twisty paths until we were deep in the wild part and Plato was gasping. I stopped and he flopped down on a flat mossy tombstone. He looked blue round the mouth. He tried to speak. "That . . . wa . . ." was all he could manage.

"Plenty of time," I said. "You may have picked the right place to die but you're a bit young for it."

He smiled weakly and fumbled for his inhaler.

While he recovered, I looked at the tombstones nearby.

They were not all for old people. Beth Blossom had 'fallen asleep' in 1910, when she was three years old. And the family vault of the Sidcup family had the names of four children carved on it. Herbert Sidcup, Florence Sidcup, James Sidcup, and Prudence Sidcup, had all died when they were younger than I was.

I thought of them lying under my feet, quiet and still. I wondered what it would be like to have such a large loving family that everyone wanted to be buried together. And I wished I hadn't made that silly joke to Plato.

I said, "You're all right, aren't you? I mean, you aren't going to die?"

He was still a bit breathless but the blue look had gone from his mouth. "Shouldn't think so. People do die from asthma. Most don't. A good many often grow out of it. That wasn't your stepmother."

"No. No, it wasn't."

"Too old."

"Yes," I said.

"Aunt? Older sister? Grandmother?"

I hadn't wanted to tell him. I hadn't even wanted to think about it. Now I was forced to. "She's my father's mother," I said. "I've seen her photograph in his cabin. Only she was younger and her hair was dark."

"You mean, she's your grandmother!"

"I suppose so." I tried to look surprised, as if this thought had only just occurred to me. I said, "I've never met her. She's never met me. I thought she lived in America."

"Maybe she does." Plato looked at me warily. Then his face brightened. "Perhaps this is her first visit to London."

I shrugged my shoulders.

"Oh. Well." He sucked at the braces on his teeth, making an irritating clicking noise. "There must be some explanation. Your grandmother has come from America for the first time, and she's staying with your father and Amy, and Amy has stopped her coming to see you. If Amy's mad

54

enough to stop you seeing Annabel and George, she's mad enough for that! She probably threatens to kill herself to get her own way. Cut her veins in the bath. Or put her head in the gas oven. My mother was always frightening my father with something like that. It didn't work in the end because he left all the same, but it might work for a while on someone who wasn't used to it."

"I'm glad you've got your breath back," I said.

"It makes sense, doesn't it? What else could it be?"

"Just that she doesn't want to have anything to do with me. Even if she did live in America, she could have written to me if she'd wanted to. Or sent me a birthday card. Not that I care. If she wrote to me I'd have to write back to her. And I hate writing letters."

That was a big lie. I would have liked to have hundreds of grandmothers, all sending me birthday cards. I would have written back to them all, long, brilliant letters so they would never forget me. But Plato hates families, so he believed me.

"Relations are a pain," he agreed. "My relations, anyway. Always ringing each other up and shouting. The Welsh ones are better than the Greek, but only because they are meaner about using the telephone. And my Welsh grandmother sends me a text to learn each week. From the Bible."

Aunt Sophie and I read to each other out of the Bible, and not only on Sunday. Aunt Sophie didn't go to church with Aunt Bill and me, but she said that if I didn't know the Bible I would never understand English literature. But I didn't say this to Plato in case he thought Aunt Sophie was cranky.

I said, "You like Aliki, though."

"I told you. Brothers and sisters are different."

"I wish I'd had the chance to find out."

My chest grew tight as I thought of it; playing with George and Annabel, taking them to the adventure playground, teaching them games. I wondered if Annabel was ever teased about her hand. I thought, if someone teased her when I was there, I'd tear their ears off.

I wondered if Plato had noticed her hand. I didn't like to mention it in case he hadn't. I was sorry and ashamed for Annabel.

Plato was watching me. He said, "If you want to get to know them, you can. We can come in the holidays. I expect they go to play in the cemetery. Or there may be a proper park somewhere. If we hang about, we could see where they go. You could speak to them."

"I wouldn't dare." I had seen them. I had heard George talking. I knew where they lived. I hadn't thought about what would happen next. I had seen them and got safely away without any complications and that was enough for the moment. What I wanted now was to go home and just think about them. Quietly, and on my own.

Plato was watching me with a disgusted expression.

"You can't start a thing and then give it up, just like that. I thought you were really interested in Annabel and George, that you thought it was really *important*. I wouldn't have wasted my time if I'd known you only wanted to see them just once, and then pack it in."

"I don't *know* what I want," I said. "Now that I've seen them, I feel a bit funny. I don't know what I want to do next. Or what we *can* do."

"I've been thinking about that," Plato said. "We can just watch the house, follow them when they go out, find out if they are ever alone. Easy enough to make friends in a park, or a playground. Or if you fancy something a bit more exciting we could kidnap them. We wouldn't scare them, just make it seem like a game. We'd hide them somewhere, and give them plenty to eat, and we could send a letter to their mother saying she can have them back as soon as she agrees to your seeing them whenever you want to. They'd be sort of *hostages*."

He was spluttering with enthusiasm for this ridiculous

plan. Because I had nothing else to suggest, I felt let down and peevish. I said, "It's only terrorists who take hostages, and we'd be caught, anyway. Sent to prison or something. I'll be in quite enough trouble if the Aunts find out I didn't go to school today. I shan't know what to tell them. I can't tell them the truth."

"You could," Plato said. "You mean, you don't want to. The truth is the easiest thing almost always, but the next best thing is a sensible lie. You just have to think yourself into it till it feels natural. That way you don't trip yourself up."

I groaned and he looked at me, pushing his glasses up on his nose. "Okay," he said. "I'll think of something. Don't worry."

"That boy is a bad influence," Aunt Sophie said.

She frowned as she spoke, but only because she thought she ought to be cross with me. In fact, she was angrier with Maureen who had popped her head over the fence while Aunt Bill was gardening. "Of course, soon as Bill asked her what she was doing at home, that young madam was happy to tell her there was no school for your class today," Aunt Sophie said, with a sniff. "Why didn't you tell us, Jane? It's not like you to be deceitful. Don't blame it on Plato."

"I thought that was what *you* were doing. He's not a bad influence. It was *my* fault that I didn't tell you we were on holiday. He hadn't told his mother because she'd have made him stay home and do housework, or go to the launderette, or do all the shopping."

"Is she as bad as that? I thought she was just a lonely sort of woman, not some kind of slave driver."

Aunt Sophie was frowning properly now. Omitting to say that I had a day's holiday was one thing; blackening a person's character, quite another.

I muttered, "Well, anyway, she never lets him have any time to himself. And I thought, if we were late home, she

57

might telephone you. And you know what would have happened then. If you knew where we were you'd have told her. You know you hate lying."

I hoped I sounded sarcastic and that she would take it to heart. Although she hadn't actually *told* me I was alone in the world, she had let me believe it.

But she didn't seem to hear the tone of my voice, or notice the piercing look that I gave her. She had stopped frowning and was smiling at me. She said, "Where did you go, dear?"

"Out," I said. "Out and about." Stick as close as you can to the truth was Plato's advice. Not that he followed it himself, I had noticed. But then he was more practised at lying than I was. "We went to London," I said. "I know you don't like me to travel alone, but I didn't think you'd mind my going with Plato. He wanted to go to a book-shop."

This was the right kind of excuse for Aunt Sophie. She said in an interested voice, "Did he find what he wanted?"

My mind was a blank. Plato hadn't suggested a book he might have wanted and I couldn't think of one. I said, "He just wanted to browse. There's not much of a choice in that shop in the High Street."

"That's true," Aunt Sophie said. But she was looking distant as if she meant just the opposite.

I thought, crossly, that Aunt Bill would have believed me!

Then Aunt Sophie surprised me. She said, "I'm so sorry to question you, dear. Bill and I worry about you, but that's no excuse for not giving you enough freedom. I'll talk to Bill about it. We'd like to know where you're going and when you'll be back, but we'll try not to pry in the future. After all, we know we can trust you."

Chapter Seven

My father was back at sea. He had sent me a postcard from Southampton that said he was off again and would see me next time. He put dozens of kisses round the edge of the postcard.

I telephoned Shipshape Street. Sometimes a woman's voice answered and then I put the receiver down quickly. But if it was Annabel or George, I hung on while they said, "Hallo," or "Who's that?" or, if it was Annabel, "Do you want my Mummy?"

Then one day Annabel called out, "Mummy, it's that person who doesn't speak, only listens."

I thought of my musical box. I had had it as long as I could remember. It had belonged to my mother and when I was small, two little drummers used to spring up when you opened the lid. They stopped working when I was five and took the box with me to school, but the music still played; a pretty, tinkling tune.

I put it ready beside the telephone. Annabel answered and I lifted the lid. She said, "Oh," as the tune began playing, and laughed when it finished, and said, "Come here, George. Listen. It's a music box."

It was a good way of hearing their voices and getting to know them as they talked to each other. George said one time, "Is it magic, An'bel?" And I heard her explain that it was one of those things like the Time or the Weather Forecast that the telephone told you if you rang the right number. She said, "I expect it's got turned round somehow." I thought that was clever and sweet. George said, very excited, "Then it *is* magic, isn't it?" And she said, sounding very grown-up, "Not really, not real, fairy magic. Just a mistake of the telephone people."

Aunt Bill and I were supposed to go to Dorset at the end of term, but Aunt Bill's friend, who had been at art school with her, wrote to say that the twins had got chicken pox badly and it would be better if we could go later on, towards the end of the holidays. I tried to sound sorry when the letter arrived, because Aunt Bill had been looking forward to being in the country, seeing her friend, tramping the hills, and painting wild flowers and berries, but I can't have been very convincing. Aunt Bill looked at me in a puzzled way and said, "I thought you enjoyed going there, Jane. You had a fine time last year. Organising those little children."

That was before I found out I had a real brother and sister. I said, "I expect I've grown out of playing families. Kids can get boring."

"She's got better things to do these holidays, Bill," Aunt Sophie said. And she winked at me.

She meant Plato. In the ordinary way I would have objected to the suggestion that I was keen on an asthmatic, short-sighted squirt of a boy a year younger than I was. But in the circumstances I could see that the idea was useful. I couldn't make myself blush, but I lowered my eyes modestly and said, "Well, we do have a few plans. Plato wants to go to some museums and galleries." I looked at the Aunts and saw they were beaming approval of these educational projects. To make sure they were both equally pleased. I went on, "Especially the Natural History Museum for the birds and animals, and the National Gallery for the pictures."

Naturally, Plato's real plans were different. "What spies do is find a house near the one they want to watch, and get in somehow, rent a room, something like that, and settle down with a telescope and a camera with a zoom lens."

I let him run on, since it seemed to amuse him and there was no one around to hear him being so childish. And in fact to begin with, when we went to Shipshape Street the first week of the holidays, the laugh was on me. There was an empty house opposite Number 22, with a builder's board up, and scaffolding, and a stack of bricks in the little front garden, although no one was working yet. There was no side entrance, but at the end of the terrace a cinder path led round the back along the ends of the gardens. To listen to Plato, you would think he had planned it. "Perfect," he said. "What did I tell you?"

"We can't break in," I said. "It's trespassing. We'll get into trouble."

"Only if we're caught," Plato said, as we marched along the cinder path. "Even then we'd only be told to push off. Who's going to fuss over a couple of little kids playing?"

He wriggled his shoulders and seemed to shrink inside his clothes so that he looked much younger, around ten, and mischievous. I said, "If we're caught, I warn you, I'll run. Leave you to do all the talking."

But there was no one around. The cinder path was empty except for the dustbins, each painted with the number of the house it belonged to. The dustbins for Number 19 were empty and the back gate swung open, loose on its hinges. Inside, the garden was jungle; apple and pear trees grown straggly so that their branches met over our heads, and rambler roses and clematis twined among them. No one had pruned them this year and perhaps last year, too; the ground was soft with the leaves of last autumn. The fences were high and although we could hear children playing somewhere quite close, they couldn't see us and we couldn't see them.

"It must have been empty for ages," Plato whispered. The windows on the ground floor were boarded and a couple of planks nailed across the back door. There was a sash window half-way up the wall, between the ground and the first floor, but there was no way of reaching it. A drain-pipe at the side looked too rusty and old to be trusted.

I had lost my nerve anyway. Peering in through the planks, through the glass of the back door, I thought the inside of the house looked dangerously derelict, with a jagged hole in the ceiling and boards hanging down. I said, "Even if we could get in, we'd break our legs probably. It's all rotten."

Plato tugged at the planks. "These are rotten all right." A few splinters came loose. He shook his head and stepped back, sucking his fingers. "I need a crowbar," he said. "Or a jemmy."

"Why don't you shout over the fence and see if next door have got one?" I was being sarcastic because Plato had sounded so matter-of-fact—as if most people normally carried burglary tools around with them.

He looked at me, very straight. "I don't suppose they'd have one, do you? But I'll try if you like."

And he actually got hold of an old plastic crate that was part of the litter around the back door and put it against the fence between the two houses. But the moment he climbed on it, the next door dog started barking.

It wasn't an ordinary bark. It was a deep, throaty baying that had a thick, wet, snarling base to it; the barking of a huge, savage hound. And as it barked, it flung itself against the fence, leaping high, so that for a second we saw a wild, rolling, red eye and a great snout, lips drawn back, white teeth flashing.

One glimpse was enough. Plato tumbled off the plastic crate and we tore down the garden, the dog running beside us on the other side of the fence, thudding against it, leaping and growling. We stumbled down the jungly garden and through the gate to the cinder path. I thought, suppose the gate to the other garden is open!

I didn't stop to look. Plato had started gasping. I grabbed his hand and dragged him along with me. Behind us, the dog's howling grew frantic. I heard the scrabbling of its paws and the crashing of its body against the wooden fence. Then a man shouted. The dog yelped as if someone had thrown something at it, and its barks became whimpers.

Plato collapsed on a dustbin. When he had gathered his breath, he said, "That was *blood-curdling*. I don't know what blood feels like when it's curdled, but mine's *cold*. As if my veins ran with ice."

"Milk goes lumpy when it curdles." It seemed an odd moment to be discussing the meaning of words. I said, "I'm not going back there."

"I expect its bark is worse than its bite. It's probably a soft old thing really. Just wanted to play with us."

"I'm not risking it."

"It couldn't get over the fence. Maybe it'll be shut up next time."

"You try, then. If it's all clear, you can light a bonfire. Smoke signals. Make sure the whole street knows what we're up to. In fact, we could send every house a round robin letter. Ask if anyone would be kind enough to lend us their front room for the holidays so we can spy on the people in Number 22."

I felt despairing. *A couple of little kids playing*, Plato had said. He had meant that was how a grown-up would see us, but it was what we *were*: two kids, pretending. I said, "It's no good. There's nothing we can do. Let's go home."

He said patiently, "There is one thing. We could simply knock on their door. If your stepmother hasn't seen you since you were three, hasn't *wanted* to see you, then she probably hasn't seen a photograph of you, either. We could say we were collecting for something. Or looking for sponsors for a walk, or a swim, to make money for charity." He giggled suddenly and sharply, "For Oxfam. Or for handicapped children."

I stared at him and he went red. He said, "I'm sorry. That wasn't funny. I don't know why I said it."

I was too miserable to be angry. I said, "I didn't think you'd seen her hand. What do you think happened?"

"I don't know. Genetic, probably. Born with it."

"Do you think she minds?"

"I expect so. Like I mind about asthma. You just have to get used to it."

"I don't think having asthma's so bad."

"You haven't got it. But it isn't just that. It's other things, too. Like being ugly and small."

I said, "Don't be silly!"

He pushed his glasses up on his nose and looked at me sternly. "It's as I said, you have to get used to it. To being different. Outside."

"Outside?"

"Looking at all the people *inside* who don't lose their breath when they run, or wear braces on their teeth, and who have proper families. Mothers and fathers and brothers and sisters. All living together."

I said, "If that's being outside, then I'm outside, too. I mean, I'm outside George and Annabel's family."

"That makes two of us." He giggled. "Like the two Bisto Kids."

It was then that he told me about this old advertisement. Sitting on a dustbin at the end of the cinder path, he wrinkled his nose and pretended to be a starving orphan smelling something good cooking.

He made me laugh. He made me hungry. I said, "Aunt Sophie made me cold roast beef and cucumber sandwiches. Enough for the two of us."

We went into the cemetery and ate lunch sitting on the tomb of Stanley Arthur McAlpine who had been 'called to the Lord' in 1925. The flat part of the tomb was grey-green with lichen, but the marble angel with folded wings that stood over it was still white and clean. There was a verse on its base.

> *Father in Thy gracious keeping,*
> *Here we leave Thy servant sleeping.*

These words brought a lump to my throat, but Plato said it wasn't so sad since Mr McAlpine had been eighty-two when he died. After we had finished eating we tried to scrape some of the mouldy green off the flat part of the tomb, and Plato pinched some plastic daffodils from a newer grave and stuck them into the earth at the feet of the watching angel. Then we looked round the cemetery for other McAlpines, but we didn't find any; Stanley Arthur was the only one of his family who had been buried there. Plato said perhaps all the others had been cremated but neither of us knew if there had been cremation so long ago.

Plato said he would look it up in the encyclopedia when he got home. He said he would rather be cremated when he died because it was tidier and took up less space, but I thought I would rather be buried, so that people could come and look at my tombstone and wonder about me.

Neither of us mentioned Annabel and George. It was as if we had each decided, on our own, separately, to ignore what had brought us here, to Bow Cemetery; as if we had both realised, since the dog chased us out of the garden, that we had no real idea how to go on. I knew I was beginning to be afraid that if we hung around Shipshape Street very much longer, something awful would happen, and Aunt Bill and Aunt Sophie would find out what I'd been up to.

I said, "Perhaps if we go soon, we really could go to the National Gallery on the way home."

I thought Plato would object. But he shrugged his shoulders. "Okay. Why not? We've found out the interesting part, after all. Where they live, what they look like. Spying gets boring after a bit."

And that would have been that, over and finished and no harm done to anyone, if we had not walked to the station by way of the grassy clearing at the side of the railway line, and seen the grandmother—*my* grandmother—asleep on a bench in the sunshine.

Chapter Eight

She looked quite comfortable, her head resting on the back of the bench, her legs stretched out in front of her, and her hands folded across her handbag on her lap. Her mouth had fallen open and she was snoring gently. A little bit of cottony stuff, some sort of seed blown on the wind, had settled on her upper lip, and it fluttered with each breath.

I looked at this sleeping person who was my grandmother, and thought how odd it was that she was a stranger to me.

She stirred and muttered something. "Come away," Plato said. "They'll see you. They'll think we're thieves. Stealing her handbag or something."

The children had come out of the bushes on the other side of the clearing. They were running towards us, a little, matted dog chasing them, leaping up, yapping. We walked slowly towards them and they glanced at us briefly as they ran past us. George said, "Gran?" and Annabel hushed him. "Don't wake her."

At the edge of the clearing we stopped and looked back. Annabel was fastening the dog's leash to its collar and slipping the loop over an iron strut on the bench. "Stay," she said. "Good dog." And the little dog sat like a statue, ears up, head cocked to one side.

The children backed away from the bench, giggling. George whispered something to Annabel and she looked in our direction.

"Pretend to be busy," Plato said. "Let's pick blackberries."

High up where they caught the sun, a few berries were ripening, but on the lower branches they were still shrunken and green.

"Rhubarb, rhubarb, rhubarb," Plato said. "That's what actors say when they're part of the crowd on the stage and pretending not to notice what's going on. If you get a stick, you might be able to reach some of the top bits. I'll keep an eye on your brother and sister."

The bushes were covered with dust and smelled fusty. The few berries I managed to reach were sour and pursed my mouth up. "*Yuck*," I said, spitting. "What are they doing, Plato?"

I was too nervous, or shy, to look round myself.

"Nothing special," he said. "It's all right, they're not watching us." Then, concerned suddenly, "Oh, *no* . . ."

I looked then. They were standing at the wire fence between the clearing and the railway line.

I said, "They're just watching for trains. All kids do that."

George had sat down. Annabel was stooping over him, pulling at something. George was on his back, wriggling. He disappeared. Annabel looked over her shoulder at her sleeping grandmother. George's head popped up on the other side of the fence. Annabel sat down.

"They're sliding under the wire," Plato said. "That's dangerous . . ."

Annabel was wearing a skirt. A bit of it must have snagged on the fence. She said, "Oh . . ." and then a rude word I would not have expected. George was out of sight but I heard him laugh. Annabel tugged her skirt free. Then she vanished too.

Plato set off at a run. I followed him, my heart jumping. I was afraid he was going to wake the old lady, but he swerved as he passed the bench and made for the fence. We stood, peering through. There was no sign of the children.

The rails started to hum. We could hear the train in the tunnel. It roared out and banged past, making the fence shake. Plato said, "We'd better see where they've got to."

He slithered under the wire and held it up for me. There was a narrow path of trodden grass that led down the steep slope towards the dark mouth of the tunnel. There was nowhere else they could hide.

We stopped at the entrance. There was room between the rails and the black wall for a person to walk, but it would be terrifying to be caught there, I thought, with a swaying train crashing past. I shivered and Plato said, "Some kids enjoy being frightened." He called out, "Hallo, there," and his shout echoed hollowly under the curved roof of the tunnel.

We waited. "Come on out," Plato said, using his deep, grown-up voice. "Now. This minute."

I thought I heard a whisper, quite close. Then silence.

Plato said, "My father's a policeman. If you don't come out, I'll get him to fetch you. Then you'll be in real trouble."

A few yards away a thin beam of light wavered, enough to illuminate an arch in the side of the tunnel. Annabel came out of it, shining her pencil torch in our faces. "It's all right," she said. "It's not those rough boys."

"I'm not scared of any old boys," George said indignantly. "I'm not scared of anyone."

This was so exactly the sort of thing I would have expected him to say that I couldn't help laughing.

Plato looked at me coldly. "It's not in the least funny. They could have been electrocuted. Or run over by a train. You wouldn't laugh, would you, if you saw someone mashed up in the wheels, torn to bits, just blood and bone, screaming?"

I said, "Don't frighten them, Plato."

He frowned at me; a frown that was meant as a warning. He said, "It seems someone has to."

"We were quite safe," Annabel said. "We always go in the hole at the side. It's a special safe place for railwaymen when they are working."

She sounded bold enough, but as she emerged into the daylight at the end of the tunnel, I saw that she was scarlet with embarrassment and shame.

I said, when they were safe on the bank, "What did you mean about the boys? What rough boys?"

"Big boys," George said. "Sometimes they chase people in the cemetery. Last holidays they chased us and one of them had a knife, so we ran and hid in the tunnel." His eyes were round with excitement, not terror. "Then they came after us, but we found the hole and hid in it, and they couldn't find us. And a train went by like a *dragon*, and Annabel cried, but I didn't."

"No one was chasing you this time," Plato said.

I had never seen him so solemn and stern. He hadn't been frightened before, when we first saw what they were doing. He had frightened himself since with what might have happened. He was still frightened now.

Unlike George, who said boastfully, "I like to hide in the tunnel with the trains going by. It makes fireworks go off in my head. It's my *best treat*. It scares Annabel but it doesn't scare me. It doesn't scare me one bit."

"Then you must be an exceptionally stupid boy," Plato said.

"He's not stupid," Annabel said, speaking fiercely. She pushed in front of George, placing herself between him and Plato. "It was my fault. He wanted to go and I wouldn't let him at first, but then I said I'd take him if he was nice to Gran and stopped teasing her. And he *was* nice, so I had to." Her forehead creased anxiously. "My Daddy says it's wrong not to keep your side of a bargain."

She looked straight at me as she said this. It was probably

only because she thought I was more sympathetic than Plato, but it gave me a strange feeling, all the same, to hear my little sister telling me something our father had said!

I said, "Isn't George usually nice to his Gran?" I saw Plato's expression and knew, at once, what I'd done.

Annabel hadn't noticed. But George said, "How do you know my name?" He wasn't stupid. He was sharp as a pin.

Plato said, "Your sister told us, dummy! You called her Annabel. She called you George."

I saw his eyes—blue eyes, like our father's—cloud over as he tried to remember. I said quickly, "It wasn't being very nice to Gran to go in the tunnel, was it? How do you think she'd have felt if you both had been killed?"

"*She* wouldn't mind. She'd say, good riddance to bad rubbish."

I laughed. "I don't believe you."

"She said it this morning when I said I was going away and never coming back. She said it even after I showed her I'd packed my suitcase."

"That's not fair," Annabel said. "You know you were being horrible about the baby. You know what you said."

He looked at her, sidelong and sly. "I said, Throw the pig baby into the dustbin if he keeps up that squealing noise. Everyone was just as fed up as me!" He put on an injured tone. "I don't know why Gran got so mad!"

Plato said, "Have you got a new baby in your family?"

Annabel nodded. "He's a week old. He's going to be christened Horatio. That's one of Daddy's names. The other one's Edward. And George has got that one for his second name. It's Daddy's second name, too, and it's the one that he's called by."

"I think Horatio stinks," George said. "I'd kill anyone who called me Horatio. I know he was a famous sailor but the silly people in my class won't know that."

"Has the baby got another name?" I asked. I tried to sound calm, though I felt light-headed and shaky.

"William," Annabel said. "That's what Daddy wants to call him. But Mummy doesn't like it. She says he'll be called Bill for short, and she doesn't like Bill. She wants Humphrey, after her father."

"Horatio Humphrey is a bit of a mouthful," Plato said.

George turned beady eyes on him. "What's *your* name? And *hers*?"

Plato winked at me. "I think we'd better get off this railway before we get arrested," he said. "And wake up your grandmother."

She wasn't on the bench. "She's gone looking for us, she'll be worried," George said with some satisfaction. "People get mugged in the cemetery sometimes. There are all sorts of robbers, and gipsies, and people with dangerous dogs."

"Kidnappers, too?" Plato said. "If you want to get rid of Horatio Humphrey, you could always leave him here in his buggy and see what happened."

George stared, his face swelling with outrage. "I wouldn't let anyone take him. I'd *kill* them."

"He didn't mean it," I said. "He was joking. I think we should go and look for your grandmother."

"It's better if we stay here," Annabel said. "We always stay where she lost us. So she knows to come back if she can't find us." She hesitated, the crimson colour coming up in her face. "Gran doesn't lose us, or go to sleep usually. It's just that she's been up at night with the baby."

I caught Plato's eye and we smiled at each other. I wondered if his sister was as sweet as mine. I said, "Perhaps we'd better stay till she comes back. We could play a game."

Plato had some string in his pocket and he taught them cat's-cradle. George was quick to learn, he only had to be shown once. Annabel was slower because of her missing thumb and forefinger, but I was interested to see that although she had hung back to start with, as soon as she

72

knew we had seen her bad hand, she stopped minding about it and was almost as neat as her brother. By the time their grandmother came running across the grass, they were both quite absorbed; tongues between their teeth, fingers busy.

"There you are, darlings," she cried. The little dog leapt at the children in turn, licking their faces and ruining their cat's-cradles.

"We were all right, Gran," Annabel said. "I'm sorry we lost you."

"We were playing hide and seek," George said accusingly. "And when we came back you and Bucket had gone."

"And I've been racing round after you. What an old silly I am! Never mind, I can see you've been well looked after."

She smiled at Plato and me. She had a nice smile, she looked friendly, but my heart was jumping again, banging about as if it had come loose in my chest. I had recognised her from her picture. She might have seen one of me.

And perhaps she had. She was looking at me. She said, "Do you live round here, dear? I'm sure that I've seen you somewhere . . ."

I thought that my heart would burst. I was dumb.

Plato came to my rescue. He said, "I'm Plato Jones. And this is my sister, Aliki."

Chapter Nine

I dreamed about them that night, and the next night, and the night after. At first, nothing special happened in these dreams. It was just that they were always there, Annabel with her sweet, anxious smile and her little hurt hand, and naughty George, laughing. Then, a week later, I had a real nightmare. They were in the tunnel and the train was coming. They were running in front of it, trying to find the safe place in the side of the tunnel. But when they reached it, the hole was blocked with a mess of rubble and the train was roaring up fast behind them, turning into a dragon with fiery breath and huge, glowing eyes. Just before I woke up, they began screaming.

Plato said, "I expect they often go into the tunnel. Annabel tries to get George to be good, and it's the best bribe she can think of. George's best treat—that's what he said, wasn't it? I suppose we should have told someone. I would have told their grandmother, except you were looking so sick, like a ten month old *corpse*, and I thought the sooner we went home the better."

"George would have hated you!"

"I could survive that! But if you like, I could ring up and pretend to be someone who'd seen them and worried about them being killed on the line. Or we could send their mother a letter made of words cut from the newspaper and post it somewhere like Waterloo, so that she couldn't guess where it came from. We could sign it *Concerned*. Or *Well-Wisher*."

"It wouldn't work. People don't pay attention to anonymous letters."

"Well, that's all I can think of," Plato said. "I suppose you could keep a watch on them all the holidays, but that might turn out to be tedious. And Annabel's quite grown-up. Even George is fairly sensible."

He yawned and took off his glasses and rubbed at his eyes. It seemed that now there was nothing more to find out, no more real spying to do, he had lost interest. We had found my brother and sister, saved them from death on the railway line, and taught them cat's-cradle. That was enough for Plato!

That it wasn't enough for me was something I was only just beginning to realise. And not just because of the dreaming. I thought about them in the daytime as well. I wondered what they were doing, and if they had looked for Plato and me the next time they went into the cemetery. And I wondered about Horatio Humphrey.

I said to Aunt Bill, "I wonder what Annabel and George are doing these holidays."

"More or less what you were doing at their age, I expect. Getting into mischief!" She put her arms round me and gave me a hug—rather awkwardly, because her hands were covered in paint and she didn't want to touch my clean dress with them. She said, "You'll see them one day, I expect, and wonder what all the silliness was about. Be a sensible girl now, and put them out of your mind."

I said to Aunt Sophie, "It's funny not to know your brother and sister. Their mother might have another baby, and I'd never know, would I?"

But Aunt Sophie was listening to her invisible Walkman and didn't hear me. Or pretended not to. She didn't answer me, anyway.

I hated them both.

★

Plato came to my house and I went to his. Aunt Sophie made a shepherd's pie and Aunt Bill picked runner beans and fat, ripe raspberries out of the garden. Plato had second helpings of everything, but when I went to his flat to have lunch with him, he ate only half a frozen fish finger and a spoonful of ice cream. His mother watched me finish what he had left and said, "It's nice to see someone eat up instead of picking, like Plato. If you came to lunch more often, Jane, I might be encouraged to start cooking real food again."

We played Scrabble all afternoon, even though it was a fine day outside. Plato's mother chain-smoked, and the stubs of her cigarettes, burning out in the ash tray, made the flat smell disgusting. Plato won six games, I won two, and Plato's mother lost every time. I thought that her brain was probably furred up with tobacco.

She kissed me goodbye when I left and asked me to come again, any time I wanted. She sounded as if she meant it. She said she always enjoyed meeting Plato's friends and that it had been especially nice to meet me.

While she was saying these things, Plato was standing behind her pulling sick faces. I thought that was mean when she was trying so hard to be nice. When he saw me out, I looked up at the window and saw her standing there watching us. She looked lonely and I waved to her. I said to Plato that I liked his mother, and he pulled his sick face again. I said, angrily, "At least she doesn't tell lies to you."

Aunt Sophie let me eat as many sweets as I wanted without even raising an eyebrow, and Aunt Bill sat with me until quite late some evenings watching television programmes that I knew bored her. And they both took days off from painting and gardening and music to drive Plato and me into the country for picnics. Once Plato's mother came too, squashed between Plato and me in the back seat of Rattlebones, and although she smoked, the Aunts didn't complain, just opened the windows.

They were being so considerate because they were sorry for me about George and Annabel. Being pitied doesn't exactly thrill me, but I could have stood it from the Aunts in the ordinary way, if it hadn't been for Horatio Humphrey. The more I thought about it, the more certain I was that they must have known about this new baby. My father would have rung up to tell them he had been born, and they had hidden it from me. Just as, until I had found out about them by chance, they had hidden Horatio's older brother and sister.

It set me wondering how many other things they had kept from me. What about all those other relations whose photographs stood on my father's desk, in his cabin? I had thought that my grandmother lived in America. Or was dead. But she was alive and in England, just a train ride away.

"Maybe she doesn't want to see you," Plato said. "Maybe there was some frightful family row and no one's spoken to anyone else ever since. My mother hasn't spoken to *my* grandmother, my father's mother, since the divorce and that's ages ago. I go down to Wales by myself now, of course, but to start with she used to come on the train with me and hand me over to Uncle Emlyn at the station as if I were some sort of *parcel*, without saying a word to him. She'd give me a letter to give to my grandmother, what I mustn't eat, what time I went to bed, and what to do if I had an asthma attack, and my grandmother would read it and laugh, and say, *Does she think I don't know how to look after a child?* And I was mad at her for laughing, and mad at my mother for giving her something to laugh about."

"I'm not angry with my grandmother," I said. "I don't know her. You can't be angry with someone you don't know. I'm only angry with Aunt Bill and Aunt Sophie."

"What about your father?"

"I'm not angry with him! There's no point!"

Plato looked at me curiously. "It's more his fault than anyone's, isn't it?"

I thought about that. I said, "He doesn't like trouble. Aunt Sophie says he's a sensitive man. And I don't live with him. So I don't get angry with him as I do with the Aunts. It's the people you live with who make you angry. You're always angry with your mother. You were horrid to her when she came on the picnic."

"She smoked in the car. I saw your aunts look at each other."

"If Aunt Bill had smoked, you wouldn't have minded. You wouldn't have *glared* at her as if she'd committed some terrible crime. Murdering the Queen, or setting fire to the Houses of Parliament."

He said obstinately, "If she wanted to smoke she should have gone in her own car. Not kippered the rest of us. Anyway, what your aunts do isn't my business."

I sighed heavily. "That's what I mean, thicko! You're angry with your mother because she's your family. I'm angry with the Aunts for the same reason. Because they ought to have told me about all the others."

He said in a gloomy voice, "Perhaps they were trying to spare you a nasty shock. Families are *awful*. When I grow up I'm going to live all by myself in a lonely cave or on the top of a mountain. I expect if you *lived* with your brother and sister, you'd be fed up with them soon enough!"

I knew that was nonsense. I loved George and Annabel. I couldn't see them, or talk to Aunt Bill and Aunt Sophie about them, and Plato was bored with them.

When I was little I had had secret people that I played with and talked to and told myself stories about: a boy, who was really a rince in disguise, and an orphan girl who had been turned at of her home by a wicked uncle. As I grew older I grew out of this childishness. I didn't forget the prince and

78

the orphan girl, but I put them away in the back of my mind, as I had stashed away my baby toys at the top of the cupboard.

Annabel and George were different because they were real, but they were secret people to me. I talked to them when I went to bed, and when I woke in the morning, and when I had nothing to do in the day. I went through all my old things and sorted out presents that I thought they would like. I chose my collection of marbles for George, and my solitaire board, and the transformer that began as a tractor and ended up as a dinosaur. For Annabel, I polished the lacquered wooden pencil box with the swing top and the sliding compartment that my father had given me, and mended the catch on the coral beads that were too small for me now. There were books like *Smith* and *The Peppermint Pig* that I thought Annabel was just about ready for, and *The Monster Garden* and *A Chance Child* for George. Horatio Humphrey was too little for toys, but I found my ivory rattle at the bottom of a drawer with some other old baby things and put it in a pretty box for him.

And, as the best present of all, there was my musical box.

I thought that I might get the drummers mended, but when I went to the antique shop the man said that musical boxes were a lot of work and people didn't always come back for them, so twenty-five pounds had to be paid in advance, as a deposit. I had twenty-seven pounds in my Savings Account, but if I used it I would have to ask for more money during the holidays and explain why I needed it and why it was important to mend the musical box at this particular moment, when it had been broken so long.

I wasn't sure that I wanted to give it to them just yet, anyway. It would be useful if I felt lonely for them and wanted to ring them up and hear them talk to each other. And then I had an even better idea. I could take the box to the cemetery and hide in a bushy place, out of sight, and play it when they came near me. They would be so surprised to hear the same tinkly tune they had heard on the telephone coming out of the undergrowth. It would really seem like magic then, like something out of a fairy tale.

I thought—I would be like the Pied Piper! Play the musical box and dance away with it, and they would follow me. I would lead them somewhere safe and quiet, somewhere no one could find us, and I would play with them and tell them stories.

Chapter Ten

I quarrelled with Plato. *What* we quarrelled about was less important than *why*. And *why* was my fault.

We went to the cinema to see *Close Encounters of the Third Kind*. Although this was an ancient film, neither of us had seen it before. Plato held my hand through the frightening parts, and as the film ended, before the lights went up, he put his arm round me and kissed me. It was a soft tickly kiss, and a bit sticky, too, since we had shared a bag of sweet popcorn. I would have kissed him back, to be friendly, if I had not heard a familiar piggy snort from behind me. I twisted round—and there she sat, Slug Maureen, entwined with a bearded male wearing a fringed leather jacket and a safety pin in one ear. He wasn't much to look at, fat and white, with red scaly patches where his beard straggled thin on his cheeks, but he was years older than Maureen.

And there was I, with the infant Plato!

I did my best. I stood up and beamed as if I was delighted to see her. I said, "I didn't see you come in. I'd have thought this was pretty tame entertainment for you." I threw back my head and clutched at my throat and made a disgusting gurgling sound. "The Vampire's Victim," I explained sweetly. "That would be more in your line, I'd have thought."

"She thinks she's ever so comic," Maureen said, to the beard.

She smirked at us. "We didn't come for the *movie*," she said, snuggling up to lover boy and rubbing her face against his scabrous cheek. She fluttered her eyelids. "Run along, children."

I could have killed her. I stomped out of the cinema, hot with shame. And, naturally, took it out on Plato.

He said, "Sorry." He looked more than usually foolish, eyes goggling mournfully behind his thick glasses, and the braces on his yellow teeth glinting.

I said, "Sorry? What for? Nothing to be sorry about that I can see."

"Oh, well," he said. "Never mind."

We walked down the High Street, past Marks and Spencer, past Boots. I could see our transparent reflections in the glass windows; a tall girl with a skinny spider-boy capering alongside her.

I thought, if he starts talking Backspeak, I'll throttle him.

He said, "Stel og rof a eeffoc."

He spoke in a high-pitched, silly voice, playing babyish, like a puppy rolling over and showing its belly when a big old dog comes near.

I didn't throttle him. I just ground my teeth.

He said, speaking normally, "I enjoyed that film. I know it's just rubbish, all that science fiction stuff, but that was *good* rubbish. I liked the way the people from space were made so gentle and fragile-looking, and clever. It was different from all those metal monsters. Do you want to come back for supper? We might get something to eat if we can coax my mother away from the idiot box and the gin. Do her good, too. Though it may be too late to stop her mind going mushy. She gets that glazed look sometimes, as if she's already turned into some kind of robot. Or a zombie, taken over by an evil creature."

He was only trying to make me laugh. But I turned on him. "Why are you so absolutely horrible about your

82

mother? It's loathsome to talk about her like that, as if you despised her."

"I don't," he said. "I don't despise her. It's just that she makes herself stupid. I mean, I know she's not clever, she can't help that, but she can help not taking any interest in anything."

"She's bored," I said. "And it's no wonder she gets bored and fed up, living with someone who sighs and pulls his mouth about whatever she says. I expect she'd rather have kept Aliki with her and let you go and live with your father, but I expect she had to put up with you because he didn't want to! And why do you go on all the time about being *clever*? Everyone knows how clever you are, because you keep on about it and don't let them ever forget it. What's clever about making other people feel stupid?"

We were both standing still on the pavement. He stared at me. "Do I really do that? I don't mean to."

"Well, you do. You go on as if everyone except you was a moron."

He shook his head and tried to smile. He said, "I'm sorry. If that's what I do. But I wasn't really being nasty about my mother. I mean, I wouldn't say it to anyone except you. I thought you'd understand. I mean, I *worry* about her. And you say things about your aunts sometimes. You complain about them."

"I've had cause lately," I said. I thought of something that would really hurt him. "And I wouldn't bother to stick up for my aunts, if I were you. Aunt Sophie says you're a bad influence on me!"

He blinked. He had gone dreadfully pale. He said, "I didn't think I was important enough to influence anyone."

I felt ashamed then. I was winding down fast and was ready to apologise and make friends. But I was too late.

The colour that had drained from his face was rushing back into it. The slanting afternoon sun shone through his sticking out ears, turning them an even richer crimson. He said, "I'm sorry. That is, I'm sorry I'm not eighteen years old and six feet tall and more brawn than brains, but just at the moment there's really nothing I can do about it."

He turned and marched off, shoulders straight, quite perky and dignified.

And, of course, I felt terrible. "Take your temper out for a walk if you must, but keep a strong leash on it," was what Aunt Bill used to say to me when I was younger and flew into rages. Most of the time, nowadays, I could manage it. I thought of my temper as a snappy dog on a leash that had to be jerked back in case it bit people, and usually I was able to stop before I had said the worst things.

The worst thing in this case was not what I'd said, but that Plato knew why I'd said it.

All through supper I wondered how I could put it right.

"You're quiet, my duck," Aunt Bill said. "Feeling all right?"

"I'm okay," I said. "I was just thinking about the film. It was really interesting. Science fiction is often rubbish but this was *good* rubbish. The people from outer space were nicer than human beings, much kinder and gentler."

"That wouldn't be difficult," Aunt Sophie said. "Did Plato enjoy it?"

"Oh, yes," I said, smiling enthusiastically. "He thought it was brilliant."

I was scared she was going to ask me what Plato was doing this evening. But after one keen glance she said, "Good," and smiled back at me kindly. I must have convinced her that all was well with my love life. Or perhaps she was too pre-occupied with her plans for the Edinburgh Festival to pay much attention. She was driving up with the band at the end of the week for a three-day gig, and was busy worrying whether Aunt Bill and I would have enough to eat during the five days she would be away, and if she had

84

laid in enough household things. She mentioned soap and lavatory paper and candles.

"We couldn't run out of all the food you've put in the freezer if we stuffed ourselves night and day," Aunt Bill said. "Even if we did, I daresay one of us can boil an egg. And what do we want candles for? Some strange religious rite? Midnight mass on the lawn?"

That would be fun for Maureen, I thought.

"There might be a power cut," Aunt Sophie said. "And you must promise me to eat properly. It's all right for you, Bill, you've got plenty of subcutaneous fat in reserve. But Jane's a growing girl."

"And you're an old one," Aunt Bill said. She hooted with laughter. "Too old to go charging about the country playing percussion. You must be the world's oldest drummer as well as the smallest. You ought to stick to the triangle! You'll give yourself a heart attack one day."

"Musicians live longer than most people," Aunt Sophie said. "Particularly conductors and drummers. It's the regular exercise. It keeps the arteries open."

I left them cheerfully squabbling, and went to ring Plato. His mother answered. "Jane, I'm so sorry, but he's fast asleep and I don't want to wake him. He's had a very bad asthma attack. The doctor had to come and inject him. There must be a very high pollen count."

She sounded friendly and bright; not at all waily.

I knew it wasn't the pollen count. I said I was sorry.

"You could always come over tomorrow," she said. "Why not ring in the morning? I am sure he will be anxious to see you."

"I'm not so sure about that," I said, and then, afraid she might guess we had quarrelled, "I mean, if he's not feeling well. Tell him—tell him I'll write him a letter."

GUSHOWI NI, MUWI (VSAMZ), KEPI.

I put it in an envelope, stamped it first class, and wrote URGENT in red letters all over it. The last post had gone, but I put it in the pillar box at the end of our road so that it would go first thing in the morning.

Chapter Eleven

Plato didn't ring back as I had hoped he would. I wanted to ring him again, but I didn't dare. I kept thinking how I would feel if he had quarrelled with me because I was so hideous to look at that he was embarrassed to be seen in my company. I would want to die. I would never want to see him again.

Aunt Bill said, "What are you doing today, my lovely?"

"I don't know yet."

"There's an exhibition at the Hayward Gallery. I thought of going this morning. Might take Rattlebones, it's not too far for the old lady, and it might amuse her to see a bit of the city. Want to come, cherry pie?"

"I don't think so," I said. "Thank you all the same."

"I'm sure the car will be hugely diverted by the traffic jams on the Embankment," Aunt Sophie said. "I'm not so sure about Jane. She may have plans that she doesn't want to share with us."

I got out the backpack I had taken to France last year and put in the presents: the transformer and the marbles and the solitaire board and the pencil box and the coral beads and the books and the ivory rattle. I wrapped the musical box in my school scarf so that it wouldn't get joggled. I waited until Rattlebones had gone farting and belching up the road. Then I stood on the landing and listened. I heard the dishwasher start hissing with water, and the bang and thump as Aunt Sophie rushed around with the Hoover.

When it stopped, I heard her quick steps across the hall to the music room and the click of the closing doors. And, in another minute, the sound of the drums.

I went downstairs and into the kitchen. I added provisions to my backpack; the end of the loaf we had had for breakfast, two apples, and a big piece of runny Brie in some Cling Film. I checked my purse to see if I had enough money for fares. I waited a while in case the telephone rang, but it didn't.

And then I set off on what was probably the most important journey of my life, quite alone.

I wasn't sure what I would do when I got there. I had packed the presents more to give myself a reason for going, than because I actually believed I would have a chance to give them to George and Annabel. It was still a sort of story I was telling myself, a game like a Fighting Fantasy in which nothing bad could really happen because nothing that happened was real.

It had been fine when I started out, a clear, blue, summer day, but by the time I got to Bow the sky had grown heavy-bellied with rain. People looked at the sky and held out their hands, and shrugged, and said to each other that with any luck the rain would hold off until evening.

George and Annabel were not in the cemetery. It was nearly twelve o'clock, and as I ate the bread and the Brie and the apples, I told myself that they were having an early lunch, too. I decided it was unlikely that they had gone away for a holiday, a family with such a new baby, and that they might turn up in the early part of the afternoon, if only to walk the dog. We had once had a dog, a cocker spaniel called Blister, who had been old when I was born. All I remembered about him was his musty old-dog smell and that he had to go for a walk three times a day, because although Aunt Bill loved him, she didn't want him making a mess in the garden.

There were more people in the cemetery than there had been before; pensioners on the benches, mothers with little children, but mostly big boys, out of school for the summer, playing football on the scuffed grass by the railway line or larking about in the bushes.

I wandered into the wilder part of the cemetery. I thought I might look for Stanley Arthur McAlpine and sit on his grave while I made up my mind what to do. I needed to gather my courage. I thought I might walk along Shipshape Street past the house, but I wasn't sure that I was brave enough without Plato.

I soon found that I was going to miss him in another way, too. Plato's sense of direction is better than mine. It was as if once he had been to a place he kept a clear map of it stamped on his mind. On my own, after I had left the railway line and the broad, open paths between the clearing and the main gate, I was lost. The smaller paths, mossy and soft underfoot and arched overhead with dark, tangled branches, were like the paths in a maze. Whichever way I turned I kept coming back to one particular tree, a dead, blackened stump, covered in ivy.

A maze is easy. There is always a rule—like keep turning right until you come to the centre. A wild place is different. You can die from thirst and exhaustion half a mile from a farm or a village. Aunt Bill told me this years ago, when we were staying in Cornwall, and she wanted to stop me going off on the moor without her or Aunt Sophie. I remembered it now, and although I could still hear the distant shouts from the football game in the clearing, and friendly bird sounds in the tall trees around me, I felt suddenly chilled.

I wasn't afraid; what I felt was only a thin shadow of fear. But it was enough to give me a warning, so that when I came upon McAlpine's grave, unexpectedly, round a twist in the path, I wasn't quite unprepared.

I didn't recognise it for a second. The boys had stuck a bucket upside down on the head of the marble angel and hung their jackets from the tops of its folded wings. A couple of the boys were leaning against it, plastic bags over their faces; two or three crouched on the flat tombstone and another lay spread-eagled on his back on the ground.

Real fear jolted me; a shock, as if I had touched a faulty electric plug. One of the crouching boys sprang to his feet with a loud, formless yell. He was swaying enough for me to hope that he was too dopey to stay upright long. As I turned and ran, another shouted, "Catch the silly tart." The words were slurred, but this boy still had the use of his legs. His footsteps seemed to shake the ground as he thundered after me.

The straps of my backpack cut into my shoulders. I was running so hard my teeth jolted and a sting of pain shot up, into my cheek. I saw the dead tree again and doubled back, not along the same track, but along another one almost parallel to it that I had not noticed before. It took me uncomfortably close to the boys; I could hear them shouting and laughing just the other side of some kind of dense, thorny bush that scratched my face and neck and tore at my clothes.

A hare freezes when it first hears the hounds after it. This was another thing Aunt Bill had once told me. I froze like a hare, still and listening. There was no one behind me, no thudding feet. I had shaken off my pursuer.

I walked on slowly and quietly, watching for twigs that might snap under my feet and roots that might trip me. I wished Aunt Bill would come, and thinking about her, I started to cry very softly. When I thought I was out of earshot, I ran at full tilt. One of my back teeth was throbbing.

I burst out on one of the broad paths where people were walking, and slowed down. I couldn't see properly. My eyes were so wet with tears that it was like trying to look through a window with the rain running down it. My throat and my chest had gone tight.

Someone said, "What's the matter? It's Aliki, isn't it?"

I rubbed at my eyes. The grandmother was standing there, her wrinkled face anxious. George held her hand. Annabel had the little dog on a leash.

I said, "It's boys sniffing glue. One of them chased me." I was ashamed that she had seen me crying. I smiled apologetically. "I'm sorry, it's silly."

She said, "Sniffing glue?" As if she had never heard these two words before. She glanced nervously at Annabel and George who were round-eyed and fascinated. She said in an undertone, "Are you sure, dear?"

It was rather as if she thought I was boasting to make myself seem important. I said, "They had tubes of glue and plastic bags and handkerchiefs. They were *wild* with it."

Annabel had gone very pink in the face. She said, "Our teacher told us at school. There was a boy in the top form *expelled*. Our teacher said if anyone tries to make you do it, you have to tell a grown-up."

The grandmother was frowning. She said, "What a terrible world you children are growing up in."

I said, "It's all right as long as you know. It's like getting drunk, people don't know what they're doing. So you have to be careful and keep away."

I tried to sound bright and sensible. Although you had to warn people, even when they were as young as George and Annabel, there was no point in frightening them. But I was feeling very peculiar. My tooth was so sore. And I felt shivery.

"Are you all right, dear?" the grandmother said.

"She looks as if she's going to be sick," George said. He made a horrible retching sound.

"Stop that, George," the grandmother said. Then, to me, "I think you should sit down and be quiet for a bit. Have you far to go home?"

"Miles," I said. I pulled a face to stop myself howling.

She said, "Then you had better come with us. I suppose your brother's not with you?"

I looked at George. I remembered that Plato was my brother. I said, "No, he's not well. He has asthma and the pollen count's high."

George said in a growly voice, "We're kidnappers. We're kidnapping you." He sniggered and put his hand over his mouth.

"Stop that, George," the grandmother said automatically, as if it was something she had to say to him rather frequently.

Annabel said, "George is silly. If you come home with us, you can see Hugo."

Excitement beat in my head like Aunt Sophie's drums. I thought, my name is Aliki Jones and my brother is Plato. Since that's all they know, I can make up the rest, like a story. I said, "Is Hugo your baby brother? You told Plato and me that his name was Horatio Humphrey."

We were walking towards the main gate. Annabel put her small hand in mine. She said, "Mummy changed her mind after Daddy went off to sea. She thinks Hugo is nicer."

It seemed a bit hard on my father. It was even a bit hard on me! I had got used to the idea of Horatio Humphrey, even though I'd not seen him. Hugo sounded a quite different person.

The grandmother said, "I'm sure Daddy will be pleased, Annabel." She spoke stiffly, as if she didn't altogether believe this. She gave a small cough, and added, "Horatio is a big name for such a small baby."

"Daddy said he would grow into it," Annabel said.

We were in Shipshape Street. My mouth had dried up with terror. We stopped at the gate. I said, "I'm all right now. Honestly. I could just go on home."

The grandmother was getting the door key out of her purse. She said, "It's up to you, dear. But you're very welcome. And you still look a bit peely-wally. We could ring your mother, if you like, ask her to come and fetch you."

I nearly said, "My mother is dead." I stopped myself in time. I said, "What's peely-wally?"

Annabel was tugging my hand. "It's something my Daddy says when people aren't well. Aliki, please come in and see Hugo."

She pronounced the name Alley-key. I said, laughing, "It's A-*Lee*-Key."

"Greek," the grandmother said. "Isn't it?"

She was having trouble opening the door. Either the lock was stiff, or she wasn't used to it, or her hands were arthritic.

I shook with impatience. Why couldn't she open the door and get on with it? And at the same time I wished I could faint and be carried off in an ambulance to a clean, quiet, safe hospital.

The door jerked open. Someone said, "Sorry, mother. Ted promised he'd see to the door, but of course he forgot it. I'd have been quicker, only I wasn't expecting you back quite so soon."

I saw, when I dared to look, that Amy was very pretty; hair thick and curly like Annabel's, and huge bright eyes fringed with long lashes. She looked at me, one eyebrow arched, smiling.

Annabel said, "It's A-*Lee*-Key, Mummy. She's come to see Hugo."

"She's had a shock, Amy," the grandmother said. She spoke in a low, mysterious voice. I thought she must be the kind of grown-up who believes unpleasant things should be hidden from children.

Amy said, with a laugh in her voice. "All right, mother. I'll hear in a minute. Annabel, take Aliki into the conservatory."

George was running ahead, and Annabel was pulling me after him. We went through the hall, which had several rooms leading off it, into a kind of porch at the back of the house: a big extension with glass on three sides and a glass

93

roof with a vine growing across it, that shed a shifting, green light. There was a red tiled floor, and wicker chairs with bright cushions, and cats everywhere: white cats, spotted cats, tawny cats. (Only five when I counted, but they seemed more to begin with.) "Doesn't your dog mind?" I asked, and Annabel answered, "Oh, Bucket *hates* them. He would kill them if they were silly enough to let him catch them in the garden, but they know they're safe indoors, so they just wave their tails and hiss at him."

She sounded so composed and grown-up that I wanted to hug her. I said, "Is Bucket your dog?"

"No, he's George's. My Daddy bought him for George so he wouldn't be jealous over the baby." She squeezed my hand and tugged harder. "Come and see Hugo."

I could see a pram under a tree in the garden.

Behind us, Amy was laughing. "Annabel, darling, not everyone is as keen on babies as you are. Aliki, take off your backpack and sit down a minute. My mother says you had a horrid time in the cemetery. You shouldn't have been wandering around on your own, but I expect you realise that now so I'll spare you the lecture. Would you like some lemonade? I make it myself, and it's rather delicious."

She sounded so kind. And she looked beautiful. I stared at her and she put her hand up to her hair. "Am I such a mess?"

I shook my head. "No. Just pretty."

She bent her neck in a queenly way as if she were used to such compliments. She said, "Thank you, Aliki," pronouncing the name quite correctly, and then, "Tell Annabel if you want to go to the bathroom. The towels are all clean, I've just changed them."

I thought I was probably too dirty to use their clean bathroom. I took off my backpack, which looked fairly dirty too, and put it down on the floor by the chair I was sitting on. George started fiddling with the metal buckle that fastened the top flap and his sister and grandmother said in unison, "Stop that, George!" They looked at each other and laughed.

"I only wanted to look," George said in a sulky voice.

"He thinks there might be a present for him," Annabel said. "He's silly, isn't he, Granny?"

She sounded so smug I felt sorry for George. He glanced at me shyly, and muttered, "I'm not silly, An'bel. Oh, I hate you."

"That's enough, George," the grandmother said, and he flung himself down on the floor behind my wicker chair. I looked round and saw him, scrooged up very small.

The grandmother smiled at me. She said, "He'll be all right in a minute."

"Not George in a tantrum again?" Amy said, coming into the conservatory with a tray, a jug of lemonade, and several tall glasses.

"He was being silly, Mummy," Annabel said virtuously.

"And you had to tell him, of course," Amy said. She put the tray on a table and picked up the jug. "Who wants lemonade? I'll pour some for George and he can come when he feels like it. Do you want a full glass, Annabel darling?"

I thought she was clever and nice, as well as pretty. She had called Annabel *darling* to make up for telling her off, and made it easy for George to stop sulking without fussing over him.

The lemonade was delicious, as she had said it would be, with just enough sweetness to stop your mouth wrinkling up. She asked where I lived and I told her in Ilford, which was several stations from Bow on the Underground. I told her that Plato and I lived with our father and mother and our mother's grandmother in a big house with a croquet lawn and a tennis court. I told her that Plato was better at croquet than I was, but that I usually beat him at tennis. I told her that we had one cat and five dogs, all Great Danes, and that I bred white rats as a hobby. Then she asked me what I was doing in Bow, and although I was taken aback for a minute, my tooth began aching again and gave me an answer. I said that my mother had lived in Bow years ago when she was young and that our whole family went to the dentist who had looked after her teeth all her life. His name was Mr Savage, and he was old now, so he only took very few patients, but he was a good dentist, well worth the journey.

She seemed to be interested in what I was telling her. At least, she kept an interested look on her face. I thought that Plato would be proud of me!

All the time I was talking, George was creaking my wicker chair from behind, but no one except me seemed to notice.

Annabel said, "I think the pram's moving a bit. Hugo's waking up, Mummy."

Amy laughed. "Oh, all right, darling. Take Aliki to inspect the miracle if you want to." She looked at me with amusement. "I hope you won't be disappointed, Aliki. He's really a very ordinary baby." She raised her voice a little. "Much smaller than George was when he was born. George was a big boy—twice Hugo's size and with a great deal more hair."

Behind me George gave a little giggly snort, quickly stifled. He was busy sliding my backpack into his hiding place, inch by inch, very slowly. I didn't see any reason to stop him. Even if it seemed a bit odd that I was carrying this collection of toys and books around with me, no one would be rude enough to say so, and it would be nice to have a chance to give George one of the presents that had been meant for him anyway.

As I stood up, I gave the backpack a little shove with my heel, helping it on its way.

"Come on," Annabel said impatiently. She was jigging up and down with excitement.

I followed her across the lawn to the tree. The baby, wrapped in a shawl and lying on his side, was looking about him with an eye that seemed all black pupil, no white showing. His tiny mouth was opening and closing as if he were a fish.

"He's beginning to be hungry," Annabel whispered. "If he wasn't all wrapped up, he'd wave his fists about." Very gently, she unwrapped the shawl, using her good hand. With her other hand, with the pink lump where her thumb should have been, she stroked Hugo's cheek.

I said, "Hallo, Hugo."

"He doesn't know his name yet," Annabel said. "Sometimes I call him Horatio, just in case. Which name do you like best?"

"I don't know," I said. "I don't really know him well enough yet."

I had a wonderful idea. If I went on being Aliki Jones, I would be able to get to know them all better. I was old enough to travel about on my own, so Amy would be unlikely to question me. If she did get doubtful, Plato could telephone and put on his deep voice and pretend he was my father and say that he hoped I wasn't being a nuisance. He could talk about Mr Savage, the dentist, and explain that I had to have a lot of work done on my teeth these summer holidays, so I would be coming to Bow several times a week. He could even suggest that I would be happy to help with the children if Amy needed a rest, or free time to go shopping with her mother. I couldn't baby-sit at night, or not late, anyway, but I could bath them and put them to bed and read them a story . . .

I wanted to laugh and jump. I was so happy, suddenly.

The wind had got up and the sun had come out, slanting over the storm clouds that were sailing away, high up in the gusty air. It glinted on the glass extension at the back of the house and shone on Amy and George in the conservatory. Amy had her arm around the little boy and their heads were bent over something that he was holding, that he was showing her. The grandmother was standing just outside the door, looking in at them.

The musical box started playing its tinkly tune. Annabel said, "That's the same music they play on the telephone."

I had been prepared for this. I said, "Oh, it's a common tune. What musical boxes often play. It's a lullaby. They play it on the telephone to send people to sleep."

Amy was on her feet now, in the doorway, talking to her mother. She began waving her arms about. George was holding the musical box close to his chest. They were all looking towards us.

Hugo began to struggle and cry. One little hand appeared, fingers snaggled up in the holes of the shawl. I tried to free them, and he cried louder.

Annabel said, "He's not comfortable. You have to pick him up and give him a cuddle and straighten the sheet."

She sounded confident that this was the right thing to do. I picked him up carefully and held him with one arm while I smoothed out the bottom sheet. He was hot and damp and wriggly, and heavier than I had expected.

I said, "Hush, Hugo. Hush, Horatio. It's all right, I've got you."

In the conservatory, Amy began to scream, a high steady whistle, like a train in a cutting.

It frightened me. I thought, I am going to drop the baby! I clutched him with both arms and squeezed him tight. He arched his back and turned scarlet, holding his breath.

The grandmother was running towards me. Her face was like crumpled paper. She said breathlessly, "Give him to me, Jane."

"Jane?"

I knew I had done something dreadfully wrong. Not by pretending to be someone else—though how she had found out, I couldn't imagine. It was much worse than that. As if I had dropped the baby. But I hadn't dropped Hugo. I was holding him close and safe.

She took him from me. She said, "There, babykins, all right, my flower, stop crying will you?" And she gave him a little shake, almost as if she were angry with him for making such a fuss about nothing, and plonked him down in his pram and joggled it fiercely. She looked at me and said in a soft, hurried voice, "What are you doing here? Oh, you silly girl! You poor, silly child!"

I said, "I didn't mean to do it. I didn't mean to hurt him." I had no idea why I said that. I hadn't hurt Hugo. It was as if someone else spoke inside me.

"No. No, of course you didn't. It's not your fault that he cried, babies cry when they're hungry," she said. And then, sounding shaky, "Don't be frightened, dear. Amy's just . . ."

She stopped. She looked frightened herself; her soft mouth loose and quivering.

Amy was coming across the lawn. She was thumping her chest with clenched fists. She looked utterly different. A stranger I had not seen before. Her face had fallen apart, as if a mirror she looked in had broken, shattering her reflection into savage pieces. Her eyes stared at me out of this stranger's cracked face. She said, "You wicked girl. Get away from my baby. Oh, how could Teddy have done this to me. Oh, how cruel! As if you hadn't done enough damage to my poor little family."

I had heard that voice before. It was a voice from a nightmare, from a bad dream I used to have when I was little, from which I woke screaming . . .

The grandmother put herself between me and Amy. "Darling Amy, stop it now. Everything's all right. You're all right. Hugo's all right. Come into the house and sit down. I'll see to everything. She's going now. Jane is going. You mustn't be angry. She's just a child, she didn't mean any harm."

"It's you meant the harm, mother," Amy said, in the same terrible voice. "It's your doing. You brought her here, you and Teddy between you, what a vile thing to do. How you must hate me."

She flung herself backwards and forwards. The grandmother held on to her firmly. Although she was old, she must have been strong. Or perhaps Amy was only pretending to struggle against her.

Annabel said, "*Mummy.*" She was sobbing, her face twisted up, hands to her ears. "Oh, please stop it, Mummy. It's not Aliki's fault. She didn't pinch Hugo like George does. She didn't do *anything.*"

"Go indoors, Annabel," the grandmother said. "Take George upstairs and watch television. That's the most helpful thing you can do for your mother. And for Aliki."

She looked at me then and, surprisingly, raised her eyebrows and smiled. Quite an ordinary smile, as if she were deploring some small piece of rudeness. She said, "Go with Annabel, dear. I'll come in a minute."

But Annabel was already running across the grass to the house.

I said, "No, I'll go away now. I'm sorry I came."

I started to cry. I was ashamed to be crying in front of my grandmother. I had always thought that if I met any relations, I would be smiling and poised and make them feel happy to know me.

"Let me go, mother," Amy moaned. "Hugo's crying."

The grandmother released her, and Amy dived at the pram and picked up the baby and sank to the ground with him. She undid her blouse and one full breast tumbled out. She said, "There my lamb, there my sweet Hugo." And then, without looking up, "Send her away, mother. Make her take that hateful music box with her."

I ran to the house. The musical box was in the conservatory, on the floor, where George must have dropped it. I thought of him, scared and running to hide, and how I had meant to be a kind and loving big sister. I found myself sobbing, deep in my chest. I picked up the box and ran into the hall. Suddenly I wanted to pee very badly.

The front door had a funny catch that I couldn't open, and

the grandmother was there, in the hall. She said, "Jane, I'm so sorry."

She put her hand on my arm. I said, "I can't open the door."

She said, "Wait a minute."

She was holding my arm very firmly. I had been right; she was strong. But my other hand was free. I undid the catch and jerked the door open.

She said, "Jane. Listen."

I said, "Why does she hate me?"

"She doesn't. Oh, dear. She was shocked. Upset. Oh, it's so difficult."

She wasn't holding me any longer. She was hugging herself as if she were cold. She said, "Turning up suddenly, pretending to be someone else. Whoever put that idea into your head? I can't believe it was Sophie!"

"It was my idea," I said. "No one else's."

She sighed and shook her head and then said reproachfully, "Well, you shouldn't have done it, dear. It was naughty!"

I thought that was a silly word in the circumstances. As if I were a baby who had dropped a sucked biscuit over the side of her high chair. Or spat in her milk. I pushed past her without answering. Out of the house, up the path to the gate.

She called after me. "Jane. It isn't your fault. Let me explain."

I looked back. She was peering after me anxiously. *My* grandmother! She hadn't known me. She hadn't wanted to know me. She would never have known me if Amy hadn't recognised me.

My tooth was hurting again. I needed a lavatory. I was very angry.

I shouted, "I know what happened! You don't have to tell **me**!"

Chapter Twelve

I knew some of it, anyway.

I sat in the swaying Underground train, my tooth aching, my bladder bursting, and watched my ghostly face jigging up and down the other side of the window.

I held the musical box on my lap, the lid open. The tune had stopped playing. It was all broken now, not just the small drummers.

George must have broken it when he dropped it. But it had played well enough before that to remind Amy of me. I had had the musical box all my life.

I tried to remember. It was like catching water. Slipping away the second you grasped it.

I was very small. A bed in a strange room. In the half-dark. There was a cupboard in the corner, the door slightly open. There was something in the cupboard, a witch, or a monster. I was lonely for Aunt Bill and Aunt Sophie. I opened the lid of the musical box and the pretty tune started playing.

And SHE had been angry. *"Go to sleep."*

That was all. The rest was just guessing. I had done something wrong. SHE had screamed. Just as Amy had screamed when I picked up the baby.

I pulled an ugly face at the ghost in the window and it grimaced back, as if it were mocking me.

At Waterloo, I ran to the Ladies. I chucked the musical box in the rubbish bin. I used the Disabled lavatory because it was free. I only had one ten pence piece for the telephone.

I thought, perhaps they know where I live! The old woman who was my grandmother might telephone Aunt Bill and Aunt Sophie!

My heart came into my mouth. At least, that's what it felt like; a lump rising up in my throat that throbbed like a heart beating. I prayed, *Oh please God, let me get to them first*. Aunt Bill said you shouldn't ask God for small things, using Divine Intervention as a convenience, but this didn't seem a small thing to me.

I hoped that Aunt Bill would answer. Aunt Sophie would ask too many questions.

But the phone rang and rang. There was no one at home. I thought that was strange at first. Then I realised that it was only four o'clock in the afternoon. Aunt Sophie was rehearsing. Aunt Bill had gone to London, to the exhibition. Although she had left early this morning, she might have gone to the Tate or the National after she had been to the Hayward Gallery. Or perhaps Rattlebones had broken down on the way home.

I was feeling more and more frightened. I had to tell someone.

I rang Plato. His mother said, "Hallo, Jane. Do you want Plato? Hang on a minute, I'll get him."

I said, "I'm at Waterloo. And I've only got ten pence." My voice had gone high and wobbly.

She said, "I'll tell him to hurry. But if you run out, you can reverse the charges." She sounded crisp and practical, not at all waily.

While I waited, I felt in my jacket. Something round that I had thought was a button was actually a pound that had slipped through a hole in my pocket into the lining. The telephone box was a new one that took all the coins except pennies.

"It's all right," I said, when Plato picked up the phone. "I've found some more money."

"Is that what you wanted? My mother said you were at

Waterloo and quite destitute. Didn't you buy a return ticket?"

I had forgotten that he had a good reason for sounding so chilly and dignified. And he couldn't have had my letter yet. It had only been posted this morning.

I said, "No, it wasn't why I rang. And if that's how you feel about me, I'd rather *walk* home than ask you."

He said, "Don't be silly."

Water came into my eyes and ran down my nose. I snuffled, "Oh, Plato, it's awful, I went to the house and they guessed who I was. And I rang Aunt Bill and there's nobody home."

He said, "If you hurry, you can get the four twenty-seven. I'll be at the station."

He was standing by the barrier. I had never been so glad to see anyone in my life.

He said, "My mother's brought the car. She'll drive you home or back to our flat, whichever you like."

"What have you told her?"

"Most of it."

"Oh, *Plato!*"

"She heard what you sounded like. I couldn't pretend it wasn't important. And it's all right. She's being sensible. She usually is sensible when something real happens."

"Is she angry?"

"Why should she be? What happened? Were they horrible to you?"

I nodded. I couldn't bear to remember. I said, "Oh, Plato, I left my backpack behind. I took all these things for the children."

He said, "Don't cry. I mean, don't cry for *that*."

"They'll telephone Aunt Bill and Aunt Sophie. Oh, Plato, I want to *die*."

"They've got to know somehow."

"It's the worst thing that's happened in my whole life."

"If that's the worst thing, you've been lucky."

"They'll think I don't love them. I told all those *lies*."

"I expect they'll live through it. But it's not what you're crying for, is it?"

"Oh, Plato," I said. "You don't know!"

"Then you'd better tell me," he said. "And my mother."

"Pandora's box," Plato's mother said. "You know what happened to Pandora, don't you?"

"She had a box that she was told not to open?"

"That's right. A Titan called Prometheus stole fire from Heaven. And to punish him, the gods sent Pandora to Prometheus with this precious box that she was warned not to open. Prometheus distrusted any gift that came from the gods, so he gave Pandora to his brother. And some people think that the brother opened the box, but I think it was more likely Pandora who was curious to know what was inside. So she lifted the lid, and all the miseries of the world flew out!"

"You mean, all this is *Jane's* fault?" Plato said indignantly. "That's not fair!"

"No, not her *fault*. Just that some girls are inquisitive, like Pandora. Jane's aunts, and her father, must have known what Amy was like, so they tried to keep Jane away from her. To protect her. But once Jane found there was a secret, she was determined to find out what it was. So she opened the box, and this crazy woman . . ."

I said, "She wasn't crazy to start with. At first she was lovely. It was afterwards, when she knew I was me, that she changed."

It was easier talking to Plato's mother than I would have expected. She had asked a question occasionally, but until she thought of Pandora she had listened in silence, sitting on the end of the couch she had made me lie down on to 'rest' as if I were an invalid. Plato was sitting on the floor, back against the wall, hugging his knees, and listening with a broody expression. I had told them what had actually happened. What I hadn't told them was how I had felt when Amy had started to scream. That once ages ago I must have done something dreadfully wicked. It seemed too shameful to mention.

I said, "It was as if she had turned into a quite different person. As if she was under a spell. Like an enchanted princess."

I thought Plato's mother might laugh at this, but she considered it carefully, as if it was a perfectly natural, grown-up thing to say. She lit another cigarette and coughed, fanning the smoke away from my face. She said, "I can see that she might have been angry. But to turn on a child—excuse me, Jane. I mean, to turn on a girl in that way for no reason . . ."

"Perhaps I once did something awful to her," I said. I spoke in a deliberately small and sorrowful voice, and then shook my head sadly.

Out of the corner of my eye, I saw Plato sit up and look interested.

"What could you have done?" his mother said, as I had known she would. "She sounds hysterical, at the least. And your aunts must have known it."

Plato said, "They ought to have guessed that once Jane knew she had a brother and sister, she'd want to find out more about them. Brothers and sisters are pretty important. Particularly when they are younger than you are. You need to know how they are, or you can't look out for them properly. And you get lonely for them."

His voice shook. I said, feeling embarrassed suddenly, "I did want to find out, but it was only *wanting*, not *needing*. It was partly a game. I didn't know them so I couldn't really miss them, could I? I mean, not like Plato misses Aliki."

"Mmm," Plato's mother said. "No, I suppose not." She was looking at me, but her eyes had gone vague and unfocused. She stubbed out her cigarette and said, "I'd better ring your house again, Jane. Someone ought to be there by now, and they'll be worried. You look so tired, dear. Close your eyes and try to rest a little."

When she had left the room, Plato said, "You shouldn't have said that about Aliki. She'll only sulk over it."

"It's true, isn't it?"

"It's not always sensible to say things that are true," he said sternly. "I know you think that I'm horrible to her, but what you just said about me and Aliki will make her more miserable than I've ever done."

I didn't know if this was true or not and didn't care very much either way. He had only said it to get his own back. He had every right to be angry with me, but because I had sent him that loving letter I was hurt, even though I knew he hadn't received it. I said, "You are being *mean* to me. I know I was mean to you, but I've had this awful time . . ."

"Poor little you," he said coldly. And then, with a sudden nasty gleam in his eyes, "I wonder what you really did to upset your stepmother."

"I wouldn't tell you even if I knew," I said. "Oh, I could kill you. I could boil you in oil! Though I'm not sure that's horrible enough! Wrap you in breadcrumbs and roast you *very slowly* over the barbecue. Roast Plato! It sounds like a *fish*."

I had almost made him laugh. He was fighting it, but he would have given up in another few seconds, if his mother had not hurried in with the news that Aunt Sophie was on her way to pick me up in a minicab. Rattlebones had had an accident on the Embankment, and Aunt Sophie had just fetched Aunt Bill from the hospital.

"Poor Rattlebones is more wounded than I am," Aunt Bill said. "Intensive care ward for the old girl, I'm afraid. It'll teach her to argue with a Post Office van."

She lay on the sofa, one leg in plaster, one arm bandaged

close to her chest, and one eye "coming up nicely", as Aunt Sophie put it.

"All colours of the rainbow tomorrow," Aunt Bill said. "Now, what have you been up to, my poor chickadee?"

I groaned. "Aunt Sophie said Plato's mother had told her. *She* didn't ask me to tell her all over again!"

"I didn't hear what Plato's mother said, did I? And Sophie was off like a bullet to fetch you the moment she'd put the phone down."

Somehow it didn't seem so awful this time. It was partly because Aunt Sophie was out of the way in the kitchen and it was just Aunt Bill listening, but it was also because telling the story a second time seemed to make it less painful. I even found myself giggling when I told her how mad Amy had looked when she ran across the lawn, thumping her chest with her fists and yelling blue murder.

Aunt Bill didn't laugh. She said, "That terrible woman."

Her grim expression sobered me up. I said, "What did I do, to make her so angry?"

Aunt Bill went on as if I hadn't spoken. "Of course, Sophie would stick up for her, I daresay. Not Amy's fault that she's extra sensitive. Some people are born a skin short, that's all. *Phooey* is my answer to that! Though you can understand Sophie. She thought she and Edward might make a match of it, everyone thought so, until this girl came along, twenty years younger and pretty as paint."

I could hardly believe I had heard this. "Aunt *Sophie*?" I said. "Do you mean *Aunt Sophie* was going to marry *my father*?"

"It wasn't out in the open. Your mother had only been dead a year, and Sophie has a delicate nature. But he came to see us, see you, of course, too, and I'd go off and dig in the garden and leave the three of you together. And I'd think, face up to it, Bill, you're going to end up on your own, without human company, only plants to talk to!" She cackled with laughter. "One thing you can say for vegetables. They don't lose patience with each other or moan and make themselves miserable. Not that Sophie made much of a to-do about losing Edward. That's not her way. She clamped down her feelings and suffered. But I knew she was terrified that Edward would realise how she felt. It was a kind of discipline to her to stand up for Amy. Or pride. You can put a lot of things down to pride."

I said, "Why did you let me go and stay with them if you didn't like Amy?"

Aunt Bill grunted as she tried to shift her plastered leg on the sofa. I fetched a cushion and propped her foot on it and she nodded to say that was better. She said, "Well, I was on my own, you might say. Your father over the moon with his lovely young wife, and Sophie determined to see only good in her. For her own sake, and Edward's. And there was nothing to put your finger on. Amy was sweet as sugar to us. Just longing to be a good mother to darling Teddy's motherless baby! Very touching. All I had against her was this funny *feeling*. And that could have been because I was so unwilling to lose you."

I said, "Did they—my father and Amy—just take me off with them? Didn't I make a fuss?"

"Didn't seem to. You loved your Daddy. You trotted off happily with him and his pretty lady. Edward was back to sea shortly, but his mother had promised to stay for a while to help Amy in case she got tired looking after you, with the new little one coming." Aunt Bill threw back her head in her horsy way and said, "Ha! That's typical Amy. Too fragile a creature to manage alone."

I said, "She's there now. My grandmother. You'd think she'd have known me."

"Did you mind about that? Oh, of course you did. Don't let it bother you. Your Granny is nice enough, but she's like her son. No real grit. No *backbone*. She rang up just before you and Sophie got back to check that you were home safely. I knew there'd been trouble, or she wouldn't have rung, but you'd never have guessed how bad it was, the way she was twittering on. Poor thing did her best, I suppose. She's scared stiff of Amy."

I said, "I didn't like her much. I suppose I ought to like her because she's my grandmother, but I didn't. She was feeble. My father's not feeble." I remembered what Plato's mother had said. "He meant to protect me."

She looked at me and held out her hand. "Come here, my chuck. Sit beside me."

I perched on the edge of the sofa and she put her uninjured arm round my shoulders. She said, in a gruff voice as if this was something she found hard to talk about, "You're a lucky child. You've got the best of both parents. You've got your Dad's kindness, and his sweet, easy nature, and you've got your mother's strength. Margaret was a fine, spunky woman. She was pregnant with you when they found she had cancer. The doctor told her there was one way she could live a bit longer. But she was determined to have you. She said, what was a few extra months of life when she could leave behind a beautiful daughter."

I thought that I ought to feel sad. But it was a long time ago.

I said, "It must have been awful for my father."

"He loved your mother very much. And went on loving her long after he was married again. You could feel it in him, part of him set aside that no one could touch. Not even Amy. Especially Amy. And that riled her. She got rid of all Margaret's things, all her clothes, all her photographs. Margaret didn't have family, she was an only child with both parents dead, so Amy packed most of the stuff off to us to be rid of it."

I thought of my torn birth certificate. I said, "Is that why she got rid of me?"

Aunt Bill didn't answer for a minute. I could hear Aunt Sophie open the kitchen door. A lovely rich, soupy smell wafted out. Supper was almost ready.

Aunt Bill said, "Not only that. Annabel was just born, no more than a fortnight old, anyway. Your father brought you back to us and said Amy was afraid you would harm her. Seemed nonsense to us, you were a loving little thing, always peering at babies in prams and asking to hold them. But you were too small to tell us what happened, and we didn't ask." Aunt Bill gave me a squeeze and said huskily, "We were too glad to have you back, chicken."

I knew what had happened. My ears started singing. I said, "I dropped her, Aunt Bill, that's what happened. I tried to pick Annabel up, and I dropped her."

Chapter Thirteen

Rubbish, Aunt Bill and Aunt Sophie said. *Nonsense*. And, *Even if you did drop her, you were such a little thing, she wouldn't have fallen far, you couldn't have harmed her. If you had we'd have heard all about it.*

I let them think I believed them. But I knew I had hurt her. What I had done was there, plain to see, in her damaged hand. I thought, of course Aunt Bill and Aunt Sophie would want to keep such a dreadful thing from me. Perhaps that was the real reason why they had never told me about my brother and sister. They loved me. If someone you loved had done something like that when she was too young to understand—thrown a stone that had killed another child, or set fire to a house—you would hope that she never found out about it, because if she did, she wouldn't be able to bear it.

I thought—*I* can't bear it.

I helped Aunt Sophie put Aunt Bill to bed, resting her broken arm and her broken leg up on pillows and making a cage for her by putting chairs on both sides of her bed and stretching the duvet across them. We gave her a bell to ring in the night and a thermos of hot milk, and put the radio where she could reach it so that she could listen to the World Service if she couldn't sleep. "I'll be fine," Aunt Bill said. "I only wish I believed poor Rattlebones had such good nurses. Off to bed now, the pair of you, and sweet dreams until morning."

I heard the grandmother clock in the hall strike the hours.
I heard all the night noises. A police siren, far away to begin
with, coming closer, then fading; cats yowling in the
back gardens; the tinkle of Aunt Bill's bell and the soft
shush of Aunt Sophie's slippers as she padded across the
landing.

My tooth began hurting again, and until it got really bad,
I was almost glad of it. I thought, this is a punishment for
what I did to my sister. If I put up with the pain and don't
call Aunt Sophie or go to the bathroom to get an aspirin,
then I will have paid back a bit of it. I wasn't sure what I
meant, but it seemed to make sense at the time. I thought of
the worst tortures I'd heard of: being buried in sand in a hot
country and having ants eat your eyes out, being tied to a
stake in the sea with the tide rising, being locked in a pitch
dark dungeon and hearing a slimy monster oozing towards
you. I thought, I could bear to suffer those things, I could
bear anything, if only I hadn't hurt Annabel.

But I couldn't even bear a sore tooth. By seven o'clock in
the morning my face was swollen and hot and my whole
jaw was burning. I cried out when I heard Aunt Sophie's
step on the landing, and she came running. She had a cup of
tea for Aunt Bill in her hand. She put it down and bent over
me. She said, "Oh, Jane, you poor darling."

The dentist's surgery opened at nine, and we were there ten
minutes early. Our dentist is terrifying, a nine-foot-tall
sadist who grins in a devilish way as he fills your mouth
with his hideous instruments. But today I was quite glad to
enter the torture chamber. And in spite of his evil grin, he
was quite sympathetic. He apologised when his probe sent
red hot needles shooting through my skull. He said he
wished he could do something immediately but that
he would rather not touch the tooth until the antibiotics he
was going to give me had dispersed the abcess. He patted
my shoulder and called me a 'brave little lady'.

★

I was sick into the rhododendron bush outside the surgery door. Aunt Sophie pushed some earth over it and cleaned me up with her handkerchief. She said, "This isn't our week, is it?" in a grumbly voice that had a laugh running through it.

Although I felt ghastly, I couldn't help smiling. Then I remembered the Edinburgh Festival. I said, "I hope my tooth is better by Saturday."

"Forget about that," Aunt Sophie said. "I can't leave you with Bill, not with her in that state."

"I can manage," I said. "Honestly."

Aunt Sophie set her mouth in a pinched, obstinate line. "I wouldn't think of it. Bill can't get around without help. And she's a big, heavy woman."

"Please," I said. "*Please*. It may have escaped your notice, Aunt Sophie, but I'm bigger and stronger than you."

It wasn't just that I knew how important the Festival was to her. I wanted to do something for somebody as a sort of penance. To make *me* feel better.

She frowned. But I could see she was weakening and that once she had thought it over she would give in altogether. She looked at me approvingly. "You're a good girl," she said.

Good girl! Brave little lady! I had my father's 'sweet, easy nature', and my mother's 'strength'. I knew that I didn't deserve all this praise. All the same, it ought to have cheered me a little, or at least made me feel less dark about myself than I had done in the night. Instead, the next two weeks were the most miserable of my whole life.

My tooth helped to begin with. I didn't have to pretend to be happy. If I looked miserable the Aunts assumed that I was in pain and didn't ask questions. Besides, Aunt Bill was in pain herself with her arm and her leg, and Aunt Sophie was busy hiring a van to take her drums and percussion instruments to Edinburgh and going to London to buy a new Vibraslap and Cabassa. And I was either going to the dentist or coming back from the dentist or sitting in his chair having the sort of things done to my jaw that I prefer not to mention. But as my tooth got better, when I was no longer writhing in torment, other things got much worse.

Plato went to America. He went without saying goodbye to me. His mother said it had all been arranged in twenty-four hours and that he had tried to ring several times. But I knew she was just being kind, and this was a clear sign that he hadn't forgiven me.

Plato not writing wasn't as bad as Annabel's hand, but it made the load of sadness I seemed to be lugging about with me a lot heavier.

I thought, if only I could remember. I must have done something dreadful to make Amy hate me so much. But all I could remember was my musical box and the monster in the corner cupboard and HER angry voice. I thought of Hugo's tiny fingers trapped in the holes of his shawl. They were so frail you could snap them like a dry twig. But if I had broken Annabel's thumb and forefinger, the doctor would have put them in splints and they would have mended.

The day before Aunt Sophie came back from Edinburgh, I thought of a terrible answer.

Plato's mother came to cook our lunches while Aunt Sophie was at the Festival. "Plato didn't want to leave me alone," she said. "And your Aunt Sophie doesn't want you to look after Aunt Bill by yourself. So it suits all round, Jane, and you'd better show me where everything is in the kitchen."

Fat lot of good that will do us, I thought, thinking of Aunt Bill's likely expression if she was faced with fish fingers and frozen peas every day. But to my astonishment (though not of course to Aunt Bill's, because she had never experienced Plato's mother's cuisine before) the meals were delicious.

Plato's mother seemed to have changed in other ways, too. She was still smoking, though not as much as she did in her own home, and she opened the windows and emptied the ash trays. She was fatter, and her skin looked less muddy. And she hardly wailed at all. She wailed when she dropped a carton of eggs on the stone kitchen floor, and slipped in the mess, and knocked a pan of stewed bilberries off the stove. "Oh, I'm so clumsy," she mourned. "It's one of the things that used to upset Plato's father."

I didn't answer this, just set about clearing up, hoping that this wasn't the beginning of a long bout of wailing. But there was only one other occasion.

She was making minestrone soup for our last lunch, chopping carrots and turnips and onions and parsnips into tiny squares. I had picked parsley and young green peas in the garden and was sitting at the table shelling the peas. A stock of chicken bones and herbs was simmering on the stove.

I asked her if she had heard from Plato and she shook her head. I said, "I thought he might have telephoned. Or sent you a postcard."

"There's still time," she said. "But it's very wild where they are, on this lake. You have to row across to the store to get to a telephone, and he and Aliki will be busy boating and swimming and talking. They have a lot to catch up on. But I'm sure he'll send you a card if he can find one."

I thought, why should he bother? I was foul to him. And anyway, I am only second best to his sister.

I said, very casually, "Did a letter come from me by any chance? For Plato I mean, before he went to America? It isn't important, just part of a game we were playing. I only *wondered*. It was his turn to answer."

She had finished chopping the vegetables. She took the stock off the stove and strained it into another saucepan. She said, screwing up her eyes against the steam, "I think so.

Would it have URGENT on it? I thought that it might be from you."

"It probably was," I said. "I can't be sure, but it sounds like part of our code. It's a silly game, really. I expect we're both growing out of it."

I laughed to show her how little I cared about letters from Plato. I had shelled all the peas. I stood up, bunched the washed parsley, and reached across the table for the chopping knife she had been using.

"No," she said. "*No.*"

I was so startled, I dropped the knife. She had gone a funny grey colour.

I said, "I was going to chop the parsley."

She wailed then. "Oh, I'm so sorry, how silly. But the knife is so sharp. I thought you were going to pick it up by the blade."

"Of course I wasn't," I said.

She smiled in a shamed, trembly way. "I'm so stupid about children and knives. Plato will tell you. Though of course you're both old enough—that's what makes me so silly. I'm so sorry, Jane."

"That's all right," I said cheerfully, and began cutting the parsley with the kitchen scissors to save further trouble.

After lunch we played Scrabble. I could only think of words that had one thing in common. Tin. Cut. Glass. Razor. Stab. Sword. Slice. Slash. Gash. Chop. Wound. Knife. All words with nasty, sharp edges.

Plato's mother said to Aunt Bill, "I think Jane looks peaky. I suppose that trouble with her tooth has taken it out of her. I hope her Aunt Sophie won't think I've been starving her when she comes home tomorrow."

I shook my head and smiled merrily.

"I'm leaving your supper on the table, ready to pop in the oven," Plato's mother said. "And there's a moussaka for the three of you tomorrow. But if you need me again, you only have to give me a ring. And of course, Jane, I'll let you know the minute I hear from Plato. If you get a letter, perhaps you'll ring me."

She said this without any hint of a sly grin or arch look. I hadn't realised before that she was really quite pretty.

In bed that night I told myself that Plato had not been able to crack the code in my letter. But I didn't believe it. Plato could crack any code I could think of. And that code was easy.

I went to bed and dreamed of knives and blood.

Aunt Sophie drove overnight and was at home when I woke in the morning. She had had a wonderful time; they had played to packed houses and there had been several good reviews in the papers. She said that Aunt Bill looked better but that I looked pale and mopey. "You need to get out and about, Jane," she said. "Plato isn't the only friend you've got, is he?"

I played tennis with Maureen. Once was enough. I rang several girls I was quite friendly with, but one had glandular fever and the others all seemed to be in remote places in Tuscany.

I said, "Everyone is having a proper holiday except me. Other girls go and lie in the sun and their mothers don't worry that they'll get skin cancer. Or that they'll have an accident if they ride a bike. Or that their teeth will drop out if they drink Coke. Why do I have to be different?"

Aunt Bill said, "Tuscany must be getting quite crowded, with half your school going there. Dorset would be emptier and rather more peaceful. I'm sorry about my old leg. Would you like to go on your own?"

"I can't leave Aunt Sophie to take care of you by herself. And there's nowhere I want to go at the moment."

I thought that I sounded noble and sad. But Aunt Bill said, sternly for her, "If you can't be happy, you might as well try to be useful."

★

I helped Aunt Bill learn to walk on her crutches. I cut the grass and tidied the flower beds while she watched to see that I didn't pull up her best weeds. I picked blackcurrants and helped Aunt Sophie pack them for the freezer. I went to the garage to visit Rattlebones and see how close she was to recovery, and was able to come back and tell Aunt Bill that her car was convalescent and would be out of hospital by the end of the week.

I had a letter from Plato. It had taken ten days to come and was creased up and muddy and torn in one corner, as if it had been caught up in a machine, or left in a sack, or dropped in a ditch. But the letter inside was undamaged.

KOJIVORI KUTI SQAKX, NKESU.

It was the same sort of code as the one I'd sent him, but a little bit harder.

Aunt Bill said, "You look cheerful all of a sudden! I knew it would take you out of yourself to try and think a bit more about other people."

Chapter Fourteen

I had two letters in separate envelopes, one from Annabel and one from George. They were the sort of letters you would expect from people their age who had been told to say thank you for presents. I supposed that their grandmother had made them write to me.

I didn't show the letters to anyone. I didn't even tell Plato. I was too ashamed about Annabel. I thought, when she knows what I did to her, she will hate me.

Plato had grown an inch while he was in America. He said that his asthma had been better there because of the dry climate and that he had been almost eaten by a bear that had prowled round the cottage at night, leaving paw marks near the landing stage where they kept their boat. And Plato, getting up early that morning, had found steaming fresh droppings.

"You can't be *almost* eaten," I said. "You either are eaten or you aren't eaten. You'd only be almost eaten if the bear had just left a bit of you, like fingers or toe nails."

I 'almost' told him about Annabel then. But I didn't. I was too afraid.

I thought that I would carry this weight about with me for the rest of my life. But there were days when I forgot all about it. Aunt Bill and Aunt Sophie bought me a second-hand bicycle, and Plato and I went exploring the country beyond our suburb, staying out all day, taking sandwiches with us. There was one good hill, the only steep hill for miles, with several sharp bends and a rubbish tip half-way down, that was wonderful, Plato said, for free-wheeling, but that needed split-second timing if a truck should be coming out of the tip when you passed it.

Although I tried several times, I always lost my nerve in the end, jamming my brakes on, dragging one foot on the road and crashing into the ditch. I was covered in scratches and bruises and nettle stings.

"You're just scared," Plato said. "When you stop being scared, you'll be able to do it."

I didn't see how I would ever stop being scared. At night I dreamed about coming down the hill the way Plato sometimes did, with his feet on the handlebars, but I was even scared in the dream, waking up sweating and with my heart thumping.

"Perhaps it's because you're a girl," Plato said.

He only meant that because girls could have babies, it was natural that they should be more nervous of dying, but the next time I tried the hill I was determined to show him. I took the first bend all right, then the next—and saw a truck turning into the tip. There was no time to be frightened. I swerved and went round the back of the truck, close enough to feel the exhaust puff hot oil on my leg. After that I was going too fast to brake and I carried on, faster and faster, swooping round the bends like a bird. It was a marvellous feeling, like flying. I turned into a farm gate at the bottom and skidded on mud. But I didn't fall.

Plato came after me, brakes juddering on the final slope, and lurched into the gateway beside me. I was glad to see that he was yellow with terror. He said, "It's not dying you have to be scared of. It's being maimed for life. Paralysed. *Quadraplegic!*"

I thought, now I've done it once, I need never do it again, but I didn't say that to Plato. I said that since I didn't want *him* to die of a heart attack, I'd be more careful in future, and all the way home I bicycled just as Aunt Bill and Aunt Sophie had told me: stopping at every junction and sticking out my arms stiff as railway signals when I wanted to turn left or right. Plato kept just behind me. Whenever I glanced back, he was watching me apprehensively. I grinned at him. I felt at peace with the whole world and light as a feather.

Rattlebones was parked in our drive, looking very well in her new coat of paint. Behind her there was another car that I didn't recognise. I suppose I thought—if I thought at all—that it belonged to the parents of one of Aunt Sophie's pupils. Plato and I wheeled our bikes round the side of the house, propped them against the wall by the kitchen, and went in the back door.

Aunt Sophie must have heard us. She opened the sitting room door. She said, "Jane, just a minute . . ." but I was too exultantly happy to hear the warning note in her voice.

Aunt Bill lay on the sofa. Her face was a fiery red plate, and her stiff, plastered leg looked awkward and heavy. Beside her, Amy looked delicate and pure as an angel in a pale, floaty dress.

She said, "Jane, dear, it's a bad time to come, I'm afraid. Someone should have told me that poor Bill had had this bad accident. But since I am here, I must do what I came to do. Which is, of course, to apologise to you."

She looked at me with a sad, grave little smile, catching her lower lip between her pretty, white teeth. No one spoke, and she went on, "I should have come before, Jane, but this was the first day I felt I could leave Hugo with Mother. I know that I could have telephoned or written. But I thought I ought to come *in person* to tell you how sorry I am for my behaviour when you came to see us. To beg your pardon very, *very* humbly, and ask you to forgive me."

Aunt Bill said, "Hmmph!" Then she cleared her throat loudly.

Amy glanced at her and then raised an amused eyebrow at me. *Funny old thing*, that raised eyebrow implied. She said,

"Please sit down, Jane dear. And Plato. This is the *real* Plato Jones, I assume?" She smiled—a mischievous smile this time and waved her hand in an imperious gesture, greeting Plato, inviting him to make himself comfortable. As if this was *her* house and she was the hostess!

I sat on the edge of a chair. Aunt Sophie gave one of her little flustered sighs, and sat on the arm. She put her small hand on the back of my neck. I could hear Plato breathing harshly somewhere behind us.

Amy's voice was soft as an evening breeze. "Jane, when you are old enough to have your own dear little baby, it will all be so clear to you. But you are almost grown up now, and I think you may understand some of it now. Will you let me try and explain?"

I nodded. I felt frightened and foolish.

Amy said, "Hugo is so little, you see. So small and so new. A baby like that is a holy trust to his mother. I know that you didn't mean to harm him. I'm sure that you love all young, helpless creatures, just as I do."

Her big eyes shone at me, bright as lamps. There seemed to be a glowing, liquid point at the centre that drew me towards it. *Into* it—as if I might drown there.

She said, "It was so thoughtful of you to bring the children a few things that you had grown out of. Of course, naughty George wanted them all for himself, but we soon sorted that out. They both wanted to come today, but I told them, another time. I had to make things right with you first, explain why I was so foolish and cross."

Amy gave a light ripple of laughter and I saw Aunt Bill frown. She said, "Rather more than just *cross*, from the sound of it."

Amy looked solemn again. "Well. Perhaps. Though you must remember that imaginative girls do exaggerate. I'm imaginative myself, so I know. I did lose my temper for a minute or two when I saw Jane with Hugo. But I was ashamed instantly! My mother-in-law said, *Forget it dear,*

Jane will get over it and Teddy wouldn't want you to worry, but, you know, I just *couldn't*. I'm like that, if I feel I've been the teeniest little bit in the wrong, I can't rest until I've put it right. I puzzled all evening over what best to do, and even though I was worn out by bedtime, I couldn't sleep, not a wink. I was up and dressed by six in the morning!"

She shook her head in wonder at this amazing feat.

Aunt Sophie said, in a queer, stiff voice, "I'm so sorry you had a bad night. I hope you've slept better recently. Can I offer you a cup of coffee? Or something else?"

Although it seemed strange at that moment, I had the feeling that she was trying not to laugh.

Amy gasped, and put a startled hand to her white throat. "Oh, how kind! I would be so grateful, if it's not too much trouble. Not coffee, perhaps, since I'm a nursing mother! Tea would be perfect. China tea, if you have it, and *very* weak, not much more than a single leaf passed over boiling water. And a thin slice of lemon, of course."

"Of course," Aunt Sophie said.

She closed the sitting room door behind her. Aunt Bill cleared her throat again. She was staring at Amy with her mouth slightly open, as if she had been struck dumb.

Amy's glowing eyes fixed on mine. I felt like a pin pulled to a magnet. She said, "Jane, there is something you need to know before you can understand. I wonder how much you *remember*? Not much, I expect, you were only little. You've grown so much since then, it's not surprising that I didn't know you. I won't ask you why you pretended to be someone else, though it *was* naughty, you know!"

I muttered, "I just wanted to see George and Annabel, that was all."

"That's what my mother-in-law said. Dear Mother, always the peacemaker!" A little trill of laughter. "But that's water under the bridge. Least said, soonest mended! It's something we needn't think about any longer. I know

I've put it out of my mind. I shan't dream of telling dear Teddy, and I'm sure you wouldn't upset him either."

"Ah," Aunt Bill said. "I thought we'd get to the point sooner or later."

Amy widened her beautiful eyes. The pink colour came and went in her face. She said breathlessly, "I don't quite know what you mean, and I'm sure Jane doesn't, either."

I did understand. But it wasn't important. I said, the words bursting out of me, "I had my musical box with me. I mean, I had it *before*. When I came to stay, long ago."

"Did you?" Amy looked confused; taken aback, as if this was something she had not expected. Then she said, "Oh, I expect you did. I can't really remember. It was such an upsetting time altogether. Not your fault, Jane. Nor mine, really. I meant to be such a good mother to you, but I was only young, not much more than a child myself, and my sweet Teddy was at sea so much of the time. And you were a headstrong, difficult child, always wanting your own way. I tried my best. I was sure I would be able to manage once the baby was born, and I had stopped being so tired and so heavy. I thought we would be the perfect family for Teddy to come home to. Then Annabel was born and *she* wasn't perfect, and it spoiled everything. There you were, Jane, a pretty little girl with all your fingers and toes, and my poor baby so scrawny and ugly. And what made it worse was that you were so fascinated by her sad little hand, always wanting to touch it . . ."

Her eyes shimmered. Tears splashed on her cheek like watery pearls. She rocked backward and forward, whimpering softly.

Plato started coughing and wheezing. Aunt Bill said, "That's enough, I think, Amy."

I said, "So I didn't hurt Annabel's hand when I dropped her!"

There was a brief silence. Aunt Bill said, in an astonished voice, "Surely you didn't believe that? Did you, Jane?"

Amy said quickly, "How could she? Jane, whatever are you talking about? Of course you never hurt Annabel, though I used to be scared sometimes to leave her alone with you. You got upset when she cried. You tried to lift her out of her basket, to love her. It was sweet, really."

She was trying to smile and to keep her face smooth. But as I watched her it started to crack, to fall apart as it had done in the garden. And behind the cracked face, there was someone else. A cold, frightened stranger.

I said, "That was when I dropped her. Not far, she was in her Moses basket on the ground, but I couldn't quite hold her. And you shouted and shouted at me. You said, *She'll never be better now, you will have scarred her for life*."

I remembered now, clearly.

I said to Amy, "Don't you remember?"

Aunt Sophie came in with the tray. She put it down on a small table where Amy could reach it. She had set out the best china. She poured the tea through a silver strainer and added a slice of lemon. She said, "It looks very pale, are you sure that's how you like it, Amy? Do you want a cup, Bill? Or Plato? Or Jane? It'll get stronger if I leave it to stand."

"Leave it to stand all day and it'll still be no more than water bewitched," Aunt Bill said angrily.

"I would quite like a cup if I could have some milk in it," Plato said. He went to stand by the table while Aunt Sophie poured for him. He was looking at Amy. He said, "Mrs Tucker, I once spoke to you on the telephone, though I don't suppose you knew it was me." He smiled, very innocently, and pushed his glasses up on his nose. "And I came to Shipshape Street with Jane, the first time. Jane wanted to see Annabel and George, and she was afraid to go by herself, even though I said I didn't think anyone could possibly mind. In fact, I thought her father would be really pleased. It must have felt very strange to him sometimes, his children not knowing one another."

This made me feel sorry for my father. I thought, if I were

126